DANDY DARKLY'S
SIX HUNDRED
and SIXTY-SIX TALES
of SEX and DEATH

Volume One

DANDY DARKLY'S SIX HUNDRED and SIXTY-SIX TALES of SEX and DEATH

Volume One

Written by
Dandy Darkly

Gaybird Press / Brooklyn, New York

This collection has been curated from Dandy Darkly's myriad spoken word performances. As the original works were intended for stage, rather than page, the author sincerely encourages you, should you feel so compelled, to read them aloud and ideally in the company of absolute strangers. Now on to the legal mumbo jumbo — this is a work of fiction. All of the characters, locations and events contained herein are either products of Dandy's imagination or just used fictitiously or coincidentally. Simply put, it ain't about you. It's never been about you. The sooner you realize this, the sooner you'll be invited to more parties and festive social gatherings. I'm very sorry, but it needed to be said.

Dandy Darkly's Six Hundred and Sixty-Six Tales of Sex and Death — Volume One
Copyright © 2017
Gaybird Press / Brooklyn, NY
All rights reserved
Cover Image Stuart Liam McConville © 2016
www.kinagram.com
ISBN-10: 0998857106
ISBN-13: 978-0998857107 (Gaybird Press)
First Edition: May 2017
www.dandydarkly.com

For Bryce. ❤

Table of Contents

Foreword

SEX AND DEATH

Sex is creation. The morning sun rises o'er the mighty Mississippi, the nimble Nile, the glorious Ganges. Mother Nature's regal rivers gush from her fertile valleys, quenching a thirsty humanity keen to sloppy kisses and lusty lapses of judgement. Naked bodies cavort amidst the churning jacuzzi bubbles of some roadside tryst that, nine months later, introduces the world to a sensitive sort of boy possessed of a pervert's penchant for carnal mischief paired with an appreciation of the paranormal.

Death is destruction. The sun sets, and six hundred and sixty-six spirits sob their sorrowful secrets from the cool side of a hotel room pillow. The bewitched boy, now a man, breeds an infatuation of unsafe spaces — precarious, unpredictable places where profanities fall from tongues like the wilted petals of some pilfered tombstone bouquet. Stolen flowers are a most fitting funereal farewell for a childhood spent eclipsed by a Southern debutante mother. It's only with a mother's passing that a dandy is truly born.

This cycle of sex and death, creation and destruction, continues unabated. We wash ashore. Eventually, we're floated back out. Until then, we huddle together. We squint into that setting sun and hope beyond hope that a special someone invites us out for a frothy folic amidst the waves — yet utterly convinced we'll drown as result.

And where the dying sun dances across the River Sex, the most magical things are possible.

The water feels just fine. Won't you join me for a dip?

Scare kisses,
Dandy Darkly

CHA-CHA AND THE SLOTH

Cha-Cha the Caveman was a Stone Age sissy, blissfully unburdened by the bluster that so defined his hunter brothers. He'd sit there — so hungry — watching as the alpha males celebrated another fresh kill, hoisting haunches of perfectly roasted sloth into the air, before gluttonously gorging themselves on tender tendon and greasy gristle. Eventually, Chieftain Gruk would get all angry, seemingly for no reason, and set about bashing a rival with his masticated mallet of meat.

Cha-Cha simply saw no reason for such hostility. Honestly? Why ruin a perfectly delicious leg of sloth?

Cha-Cha wanted sloth.

Well, one night Cha-Cha had had enough. He flounced to the fire pit, throwing his hands together to create captivating shadow creatures that scurried across the cavern walls while he regaled them all with tales of heroic hyperbole. Like how Gruk killed that very beast. How he slew the sloth — as it *slept* — singlehandedly slaughtering the stupidest, the slowest, the sleepiest critter of the Stone Age.

"Round of applause for brave Gruk. All hail, Sloth Slayer!"

Every mono-brow looked to Gruk for a reaction — who burst into laughter. He forgot whatever challenger he'd just battered and tossed Cha-Cha his gnarly leftovers. Sloth never tasted so sweet.

Born on that fateful day was humanity's first jester, our first storyteller, our first prophet, proselytizer, poet, addict, hacker, delinquent — *genius?* With a single gesture, Cha-Cha made mythology. (He also invented dinner theater. You win some, you lose some.) His belly full, Cha-Cha shimmied inside a subterranean crawl space, a safe place he often fled when the ruffians got to looking for targets for their aggressions.

Cha-Cha's sacred room was lit up by luminous mushrooms that shimmered every shade of emerald, azure and jade. Cha-Cha broke off a bit of fulgent fungus and chewed quietly. The mushroom worked its charms. Cha-Cha's bedrock bedroom became a ghostly green screen upon which his most imaginative visions could be cast — a beautiful blank slate where time existed as both the ancient past and the far future — and Cha-Cha the Caveman dreamed of wondrous worlds utterly unlike his own.

2.

HOMESICK

Apollo graced the eastern horizon. Peach and apricot splendor sparkled against an expansive stretch of virgin snow. A dark dimple marred that otherwise pristine polar plain, like some banal beauty mark slapped across an old queen's powdered cheek.

The dark mark was a cavern, a sinister crevasse whose jagged stalactites hung like fangs, threatening to devour any damned soul vexed to venture within. Yet from that hell's mouth emerged a solitary silhouette — a girl, shockingly skinny, seemingly no older than sixteen. She shivered like a shadow puppet, twig stick legs and jutting hipbones — her alabaster arms blotted with blue green bruises.

This waif wore nothing more than a beaded black cocktail dress, expensively embroidered with ornate spiders and scarlet roses, red as her bloodshot eyes crusted round with morning-after mascara. And in her hand perched an iPhone, encased inside resplendent rubies and broken babies teeth.

That fucking sun stung like a cat o' nine tails. The girl fished for her sunglasses, fumbling her cell phone where it shattered into a cackling murder of crows that flapped frantically back to the cruel cavern from which this maiden had emerged only a few moments earlier for her wintertime walk of shame.

Persephone, the goddess of the underworld, placed one petite toe into the snow, and where once a blizzard bellowed now bloomed a verdant field of green. Persephone, the goddess of spring, was home.

"Persephone!"

The first cacophony to accompany the arrival of spring was Persephone's hysteric mother. Demeter frantically attended to her daughter. "Oh Sephy, you're safe, and you're home!"

Sephy's pickled brain pulsed with a migraine — the end result of a raucous night popping pills and slamming needles. Recollection of the bawdy affair nearly caused Sephy to expunge right there. But no! She would not give her mother the pleasure of seeing her sick. Persephone was a far more pernicious party girl than times past. Like that first time, when she'd barely crawled from that hellish cave, drunken and stoned.

Demeter scolded her, "Wipe away that frown, young lady. The guests are arriving. Flowers on tables. Oh, what a beautiful day for a springtime baby shower. Hello, everyone. Welcome!"

Demeter's delirious demeanor always divulged her deepest fears, "My junkie daughter is home, everyone. The goddess of flowers is a prostitution-whore. Just smile, and whatever you do, for my sake, do not mention Hades."

For her mother's sake, Persephone played along. She clapped, and the festivities overflowed with floral arrangements: carnations, babies breath, delightful daisies. All utterly adorable and apropos for the oh-so-so joyful arrival of another bouncing, baby — *bastard*, undoubtedly fathered by any number of Sephy's uncles or cousins. Another girl charmed and chased — *and raped.* Today's lucky mommy was luscious Leda. How she sobbed as she unwrapped her porcelain rattles and pastel binkies. The proud papa none other than Sephy's own absentee father: Zeus, the King of the Gods — disguised as a fucking swan. He'd bird fucked her.

Asshole.

"You're gonna have a baby brother or sister." Demeter gleefully whispered.

Ugh.

Persephone felt sick. How could her own mother be so complicit in all this? Sephy pouted as Apollo pranced across the summer sky.

There's one mythological yarn you'll never hear among the learned scholars of Cambridge and Columbia — the tale of the flower and the sun. How the two seemed such a perfect fit. Flowers are content to admire the vainglorious preening of the sun all day long. And how she'd begged her father to marry her to Apollo — beautiful, sunny Apollo.

"Please, Daddy? If not Apollo, anyone. Anyone but *him*..." Her creepy uncle who smelled of formaldehyde and cemetery dirt. Persephone couldn't help but chuckle to herself — silly scribblings in a flower girl's notebook.

"Sephy honey, we're late for the wedding. Hurry!"

Ugh. The next event on Persephone's tour of misery was a hometown wedding. Persephone clapped, and white roses, hydrangeas, lavender garlands gushed across every surface. Immortals love themselves a big, fat, Greek wedding — celebrating another nuptial atop their insidious, incestuous little mountain. Grown-assed goddesses squabbling like children over seat placements and golden apples. All air kisses *("Mwah! Mwah!")* and syrupy sympathy to Persephone's face. "Welcome back, Sephy. So good to see you..."

And then barely out of earshot, "The wisest course of action would have been to fight Hades off. I would have." Oh Athena, so smug in her asinine assumptions. Next to chime in was athletic Artemis sincerely suggesting she simply should've out run him. Run where? She'd been kidnapped — to Hell! And lastly, pretty Aphrodite, the goddess of beauty so ugly on the inside, "Well, at least somebody *did it*. I mean honestly. She's so… frumpy."

Frumpy? *Bitch!* Persephone was fucking royalty — Empress of the Underworld — Doyenne of the Damned! She channeled rage behind her Chanel shades — fury unbefitting the goddess of spring, but most befitting Hades' queen. She snapped, and posies and petunias atrophied. In their wake awoke poison pitcher plants and vicious fly traps. A sickening carrion flower unfurled its blackened blossom. Not even its foul stench could mask the stink of this grotesque charade!

"Ouch!"

Demeter pinched her beneath the table. Sephy stormed from the wedding, a parade of profanities and shattered stemware in her wake. The only thing louder than Persephone's exit was Aphrodite's laughter.

Sephy ran. She ran until she found herself at a funeral. Apollo now fell far to the West. He set the autumn trees ablaze with brilliant reds and bittersweet pumpkin. A mother wept for her murdered children. Persephone bequeathed the bereaved a beautiful bouquet of black lilies.

It'd only taken Sephy a thousand years (maybe less) to realize that marrying Apollo would have been, literally, a fate worse than Death — the boredom alone. Not to mention Apollo's flitting after every fit young hero with a magic sword and buns of steel. How embarrassing! Far more embarrassing than being slut shamed by *The Real Housewives of Olympus*. No.

It was there — down in the Underworld, amidst the fossils and the forlorn, where Sephy truly found herself. The flower, taken for granted above, was cherished below. Never abused. Never broken. Hades doted upon his Queen like some exotic Amazon orchid. Persephone was a flower that required darkness to fully blossom.

A long black hearse pulled up adjacent the funeral. An impossibly Slenderman lurched from behind the steering wheel. Chiron opened the rear door for his mistress. Winter flurries fell softly as Sephy slid inside.

Hades, the fearsome Lord of the Underworld, awaited her return. He wore a soiled jockstrap and a leather gimp mask! He whimpered like a puppy and presented her a sterling silver tray holding a flute of champagne and a freshly pulled syringe. She forced his face to the floor with her dirty foot. Persephone sipped her bubbly while her husband groaned with ecstasy.

It was so good to be home.

3.

BLOODMOTHER

Once upon a time, in the far away land of Africa, a baby boy was born. His name was Tik-Tok, and he had three arms. His terrified teenage mommy, practically like a virgin herself, cherished those few remaining moments with her charcoal cherub. A goddess, you see, had arrived in the village — a succubus, capricious and fickle — a shape changing siren known the world over for her whim of *reinvention*.

A goddess had arrived to participate in the contemporary slave trade of accessory celebrity babies, and there was nothing the young mother could do to stop her. A sinewy silhouette cast shade into the hut. It fell upon Tik-Tok. Bye-bye, baby.

And the teenaged mommy screamed!

Once upon a time, there was a doughy Italian maiden from a dying city of industry. A calzone cheeked Cassandra — the first to prophesy our contemporary concept of "pop celebrity". She pleaded her papa not preach as she boarded a bus for the big city.

A discothèque discovery led to danceable ditties on the music TV. Wannabe's expressed themselves wearing her ceremonial couture of boxer shorts and fishnets, leather jackets with jelly bracelets. And writhing in her wedding gown, that visionary vixen from that hardscrabble town anointed herself the high priestess of the cult of pop culture. And the Bloodmother was born!

Once upon a time, the Bloodmother ransacked sissy subcultures for their creative inspiration, such as the glittery gladiatorial galas of Harlem's fiercest fighting families. The Bloodmother slapped a coat of white paint on anything she deemed sellable. She stole it away. Called it her own. Made it *vogue*.

She single-handedly killed the radio star, but in doing so she'd inadvertently devised her own demise. She could not compete with the relentless point-and-click of the remotely controlled consumer accustomed to content on-the-spot. To keep pace with the waning attention spans of her fickle fans, the Bloodmother burned through identities hot and fast: actress, bombshell, cowgirl, cheerleader, director, divorcee, dominatrix, fag hag, philanthropist, slut, empowered slut, slut-slut, even a fucking valkyrie. (Just to name a few.) *What was* was quickly trumped by *what's next?* The Bloodmother was desperate.

Once upon a time, she bathed in the blood of her backup singers.

Once upon a time, she explored *La Isla Bonita* in search of the fabled fountain of youth.

Once upon a time, she delved deeper and deeper the darkest mysteries of Catholicism, Kabbalahism and narcissism, all in search of something — *anything* — to assuage the incessant disinterest of a distracted Internet Age. To no avail.

Until…

Once upon a time, there was a boy-wizard. He possessed the voice of an angel and the fleetest of feet that whisked him across every world stage, even eventually walking him across the moon itself. His fans were legion, and anything his heart desired — no matter how bizarre (or young) — was but a fragile whisper away. Anything was his, except a proper childhood. So he shaved the man away, a fraction of an inch by a fraction of an inch. He stuffed himself full of silicone and hundred dollar bills, and stitched himself up like brand new.

The Scarecrow King became a recluse, *never-never* leaving his forever fairground of rotten cotton candy and creaking carousels. Where a mocking mug shot marked a smooth criminal, and a jeering voice barked the main attraction. "Step right up, kids. Step right up. Come see The Man With No Nose!"

On the eve of his own reinvention, the Scarecrow King mysteriously perished; his secret plans stolen from his mansion. And though he died a freak, the world would forever remember him. And how the Bloodmother hated him for that, because…

Once upon a time, the Bloodmother murdered the Scarecrow King and made away with the plans for his grand comeback. She followed his arcane instructions, scouring the globe in search of the most special (the most freaky) boys and girls — like three armed Tik-Tok from Africa — to help shepherd in what would now be her most miraculous reinvention.

The Scarecrow King's directions were a *gooble-gobbled* garble of flowery hearts and smiley faces scrawled alongside Satanic pentagrams and drops of blood. She ignored his cursive missives to "love the children," instead openly mocking them, calling them God's little mistakes and reminding them how the Scarecrow King had forgotten all about them. *Tsk-tsk, Bloodmother.*

It was Halloween night. The Bloodmother was now a crone, a hunched and haggard husk of her former glory. She followed the Scarecrow King's final note by rote, shaking a suitcase full of the Elephant Man's bones and burning in effigy a blazing taxidermy of Bubbles the chimpanzee. And from the shadows of her conjuration chamber, the Bloodmother's changelings limped and gimped in unsettling unison. They gathered in closely around their mommy-direst.

Were they holding — *weapons?*

No matter. No matter! The Bloodmother had no time for such distractions.

She drowned her world with a disposable Dixie cup of *Jesus Juice* and began to slow jam a juddering jig — a staccato slap and slide — with zombie hands side-to-side — the Scarecrow King's indisputable dance of the dead.

The Bloodmother fell to the floor, convulsing and cackling where she lay. The sound of a stadium's hand slapping started quietly at first, like soft rain tapping a tin roof. But soon it grew into a thunderclap loud enough to shake the heavens. Oh, how she'd forgotten the addictive allure of applause. The children joined in around her, stamping their feet, clapping their hands. The reinvention incantation seemed to be working. The sound subsided. The Bloodmother lay there, momentarily, before reaching for a mirror to admire her latest look.

And — nothing? Nothing!

The Bloodmother remained a haggard, old crone. She frantically flipped through the Scarecrow King's grimoire.

Had she missed something? (Yes, indeed she'd missed something.)

The fastest of the siblings to attack was also the fuzziest. Furry from head-to-toe, and formerly forced to fight feral foxes in his hometown of Chihuahua, Felipe the Mexican Chupacabra Boy, furiously knifed his Bloodmother's beefy thigh. She screamed, the rare flash of fear reflected in the boy's bloodied blade.

This hadn't been part of the Scarecrow King's plan — *or had it?*

Born bright red with rubbery skin, Annika the Swedish Fish Girl had been the top draw at the *Stockholm Seaside Sideshow* before the Bloodmother fished her away, hook through cheek. Now she made an even bigger splash, dousing the Bloodmother with an acid bath.

Yang and Yin were Taiwanese Siamese twins attached — at the lungs. A nasty cigarette habit made them both instantly Internet famous, because what's more adorable than a smoking Asian baby? Two smoking Asian babies — with acetylene torches. The conjoined cuties giggled gaily while burning the Bloodmother's blond ambition black via immolation.

Puny Penny the Pinhead Princess had once been an actual British heiress, but her misshapen melon was deemed unfit to wear any crown. Though still the

Bloodmother mocked her with minuscule scepters and royal gowns. Penny's revenge was pumping poison into the Bloodmother's shallow cheeks and cleft chin.

And lastly, little Tik-Tok, that three-armed tyke taken from his thatched roof hut, his task was simplest, but most crucial. With a razor blade in each hand — one-two-three — he leaned in and with one-two-three delicate cuts removed a minuscule triangle of cartilage — the orifice formerly known as the Bloodmother's nose.

Once upon a time — for the final fucking time — some overexposed, irrelevant celebrity (who no one remembers today) — bitch died! She died horribly. Her children gathered hands over the corpse and began to sing. They sang a curious ditty in devotion of abject aberration.

They sang, "One of us. One of us. Gooble gobble. Gooble gobble."

The corpse lay completely still. Every muscle removed to reveal the bones beneath.

"We accept her. We accept her. Gooble-gobble. Gooble-gobble."

An acid soaked arm suddenly spasmed — a beat it motion like some wanking orgasm.

"One of us. One of us. — Gooble gobble. Gooble-gobble!"

A face of death — *gasp!* — inhaled a breath. Such a thriller with lips swollen fat from chemical fillers.

"We accept him! We accept him! Gooble gobble! Gooble gobble!"

And carved from the cocoon of a gullible goddess beguiled by her obsession with unobtainable reinvention, a familiar monarch unfurled his long and bony arms. A frightfully freaky face — with no nose — turned to greet the cheering children who danced at his feet. He petted the heads of his deformed darlings whose sleeping visions he'd visited night-after-night with promises of eternal playtime and all the Halloween candy they could eat if only they commit a teensy bit of matricide.

He taught them the ancient rhyme of their kind, a phrase passed down since antiquity, a chant to embolden emotions when faced with genetic adversity. When the ordinary, the boring, the two-armed, two-legged, round-faced gawkers gape and stare, jostle and squabble — simply sing, "Gooble gobble. Gooble gobble!"

That Halloween night his children danced his juddering jig — that staccato slap and slide — with zombie hands side to side — their dear ole daddy's indisputable dance of the dead. And they sang of his royal reincarnation. The cult of pop culture's most magnificent reinvention. A song the world would forever sing.

The glorious return of the Scarecrow King!

4.

SILVER DOLLAR

The full moon hung heavy atop the desert oasis, like some opalescent apple, ripe and ready to be plucked from paradise. Bravo Team — camouflage and night vision goggles — rifles at the ready — sprinted silently across the shifting sands. In a clearing, a dozen or so handsome men socialized fully nude. They laughed. They fucked. They danced to radio disco. Their olive-wood skin glistened behind a flickering bonfire where roasting lamb let off a mouthwatering aroma. Intel had informed the soldiers these men were the enemy, but their bacchanalian orgy seemed to suggest differently. Nonetheless, orders were orders.

Pop — Pop — Pop-pop-pop.

Their disco dancing became a bloody ballet; a spray of crimson confetti and tracer fire the color of claret. Black eyes blinked yellow in the night. Rows of razor teeth appeared behind bushy beards. Fingers formed daggers — digging into the sand — launching into the air a slashing, gnashing frenzy of fur, claws and teeth. Bravo Team's screams became gurgling, gruesome gasps followed by the celebratory howling of wolves.

Otis Moonshine awoke with a startled rebel yell that rattled the vinyl walls of his manufactured mobile home. He scanned the sardine can caravan he shared with his wife — Becca — babies betrothed at twenty, but six years later, still bereft of babies themselves. In place of poolside piña coladas, Otis Moonshine's honeymoon had been deployment as an elite American sniper, peering through gunpowder periscopes, waiting and watching, then *pop-pop-popping* — ensuring another insurgent his *seventy-two virgins*.

Otis Moonshine was an American hero. Until the night of that unassuming oasis mission — and everything went to shit. He fled the firefight. He was discovered days later, dehydrated and delirious, babbling about werewolves and how his lucky silver dollar coin kept him safe from the circling shape-shifters. He was discharged. Disgraced. Stripped of the support network designed to help veterans return from war. He'd escaped with his life. Only to be tossed to the wolves once more.

Otis's American nightmare always fell following a full moon — always the same. He stumbled from that desert oasis on to a forest path paved with discarded condoms. The off-road rubbers were pressed deep into the Georgia red clay. They pop-pop-popped their creamy middles like mayonnaise packets. Night owls hooted a haunting serenade, and from behind a gnarled knot of kudzu vines chimed an orgy melody of grunts and moans. He now saw himself, the Beast unleashed, gorging on a feast of phalluses. A white-hot geyser gushed across his guzzling goatee. Green eyes earthbound, he winked his brown eye skyward, and the stars twinkled right back. He felt a pelt of fur form across his naked body as he bayed at the moon.

And he'd awaken, weeping, while his wife tried to sleep, her head buried beneath her pillow. Too many mornings Otis spent shamefully disheveled. There was no longer denying the sad fact. Otis Moonshine was becoming — a werewolf.

Otis returned from war triggered by even the slightest reminder of that terrible mission: a car backfire, the barking of a dog, Lady Gaga! He was convinced werewolves were everywhere — and they were. They most certainly were.

Every sitcom suddenly showcased some obligatory limp wrist werewolf — a neighbor or coworker swishing and sassing like some lycanthrope stereotype. The wife's hairdresser, Blair, practically oozed werewolf as he breezily thanked Otis for his service to their country and brazenly suggested Otis audition for the little theater production of *Into The Woods* — as the Wolf!

The worst (the absolute worst) were the werewolf weddings, legal now in every fucking state — and not just courthouses, but in churches. *Werewolves in churches.*

Many a night Otis spent idling outside their local watering hole. There he'd sit, waiting and watching, flipping his lucky silver dollar as they pranced proudly past his pickup truck. How these werewolves so easily showed affection for one another, slipping fingers through belt loops to pull one another into the shadows to share a cigarette or a casual kiss. The door would open, and from inside a siren song would shake Otis through the steel and glass. Tapping. Thumping. Stirring. Beseeching the Beast shred his clothes and, at long last, join his pack of burly beefcakes barely glimpsed before — slamming shut. Leaving Otis to stew silently as he stroked his weaponry: an arsenal of automatic rifles, handguns and boxes brimming with silver bullets.

Tonight.

Tonight, the mission was a "go." Tonight he would not abandon Bravo Team. Tonight he'd kill every fucking last one of them. *Pop. Pop — Pop!*

"Otis Moonshine, is that you?"

It was Blair, the wife's hairdresser. He approached the pickup. Otis hid the guns beneath his jacket and sat quietly.

"Otis Moonshine, I can see you in there. And I've seen you out here before. Listen buddy, everybody's welcome inside. Why not let me buy you a beer? It's gotta be awful lonely out here."

His cover compromised, the mission had to be aborted. Otis peeled from the dusty parking lot leaving hairdresser Blair waving goodbye in the rear view mirror. That night was spent like so many others, rambling along lonely country roads lit by Luna's glow. Fleeing his marriage of misery to a wife he loved, sure, but just barely. On to the motorway and the mileposts commenced their inevitable countdown to full moon cruising followed by another sorrowful sunrise.

Six months passed. Otis now wallowed in a sadness deeper and darker than a Kentucky coal mine. He lost his job at the prison; drunk at work. Nervous passersby avoided him on Main Street, crying wolf about the monsters among them. Even his wife abandoned him to rot in that aluminum coffin of crumpled beer cans and fast food wrappers. His belly threatened to *pop-pop-pop* the buttons off his military dress uniform as he forlornly fellated the business end of a sawed off shotgun. His finger grazed the trigger.

The phone rang — answering machine: "Otis Moonshine, pick up. It's Blair. *Again...* Well, you probably heard — I'm getting married today. Crazy, right? Listen, I know it's last minute, but I'd love you to be there. I know coming home was real tough. It's just — I don't know — you've been on my mind lately. I sure miss you."

Otis now idled outside that small town gay bar where the wedding was already underway. A pink limousine was all dolled up with rainbow flags and shaving cream calligraphy that read, "Blair and Fernando 4ever." Otis sat there — waiting and watching — flipping his lucky silver dollar with one hand. Stroking his rifles with the other.

Going to war had been the easiest thing in Otis Moonshine's life. There was no confusion because everything was simplified to one choice or the other — a win or a loss — a miss or a kill — a friendly or an enemy.

But there's only so many times another "terrorist with a bomb" turns out to just be a farmer with a bucket. Or another's buddy's legs are torn clean off — right where you almost stepped. That eventually win or loss — friendly or enemy — it all becomes incredibly murky, seemingly no more arbitrary than the flip of a coin. Could it be that simple?

Heads: he'd return to war. He'd march down that aisle guns blazing, exterminate every cocksucker that tempts the Beast at every turn.

Or tails: he'd finally (finally) surrender. Wave a rainbow flag and toast the only man who'd ever made him feel more than just some piece of dumb white trash.

Otis Moonshine allowed a long ago memory to linger longer than usual. It was a happy memory. One of him and Blair, pimple plastered teenagers playing magic tricks, rolling that very silver dollar across their knuckles followed by chuckles and awkward kisses.

Heads or tails.

Love or war.

Otis Moonshine flipped the silver dollar.

5.

LITTLE SALLY'S BIG PUSSY

Little Sally was freshly seventeen years of age. Pretty and petite. Curvaceous and vivacious with an old fashioned fascination for vintage inventions. As such, Little Sally absolutely adored her local charity shop. There she'd sit, scouring for hours in search of moldy magazines, chipped china and forsaken fart-filled futons. *Yuck.* Yet Little Sally never once purchased, bought or bartered for a single thrift store discovery. You see, she was less shopaholic and more kleptomaniac.

Oh yes, Little Sally had learned long ago the secret to stealing a tiny trinket was simply tucking it inside — her pussy.

Perhaps at this point you're thinking to yourself, "What's so special about this *Little Sally's big pussy?* I shoplift using my genitalia all the time."

And indeed, if that were merely the case, then I'd agree with you most wholeheartedly, but rest most assuredly that Little Sally's big pussy was — a gynecological gateway. A vaginal vortex. A cosmic coochie spanning space and time! And Little Sally knew this fantastical fact — and holy shit did she take advantage of that.

She started out small, stealing a pen made of copper, careful the shopkeeper not know she's a robber. Emboldened, she stole a guacamole bowl carved of granite and a busty bust of Mae West — can you stand it?

Left and right felonious fistfuls flew from sight as Little Sally stuffed her muff with misbegotten merchandise: from "aardvark" to "Zimbabwe" of dusty encyclopedias — tubas, oboes, violas, pianos, the whole fucking orchestra — more and more she hoarded into her hoo-ha until the thrift store was stripped of everything: shelving and racks, carpeting and stacks — everything. Every goddamned thing not nailed down — gone. *Gone!*

Now it should come as no surprise that Little Sally's dear old daddy did not approve of his princess purloining using her loins. Oh yes, he was well aware of her furry taco thievery. A daddy becomes keenly attuned to his little girl's hot-box once she blossoms. He was a very successful businessman, you see, and understood the value of a young lady's indisposed dewy rose. After all, what family of pedigree would ever seek Little Sally a foal to filly if her cooter reeked of knick-knacks and bric-a-brac?

None. That's who.

So Daddy dragged Little Sally to her childhood physician, a leering old coot named Doctor Fingers, to determine if she be fit to be wed and be bred. Doctor Fingers giddily groaned, "Oh my, Little Sally, how you've grown. Remove your lace panties, please." (Gross.) The doctor's horizontal smile matched her vertical one as he leaned in to examine her.

Then he was gone!

"What the fuck, Little Sally?" Bellowed Daddy. Little Sally sat coquettishly as her nervous daddy crept in closely to peek and see where the good doctor could possibly be.

And he too was swallowed fully!

Daddy awoke inside an amazing world — a womb so wondrous he didn't wish to leave. And Doctor Fingers was there, and other men too. Army men, clergy men, businessmen, politician-men — old white men who now pranced on parade. Free of the chivalrous charade they'd been forced to maintain outside this brand new world. Inside Little Sally's big pussy they could enforce their own rules without repercussion!

They renamed Little Sally's big pussy the Old Boys Club!

Next, they declared the Old Boys Club was *Men Only!* No women allowed — no pets — no babies too; not that there were any babies. Daddy was relieved to discover she'd been perfectly chaste, but if there had been babies — outta there! This is unless, of course, Little Sally wanted the babies outta there, in which case — absolutely not. The innocent, gentle babies must stay.

Men and their fucking rules.

The old boys needed toys for their new clubhouse. Faster than you can say midlife crisis they had Little Sally shoplifting all manner of macho gizmos. They started out small with erectile pills. Seeing your mate fully inflate is such a hetero thrill. Then shot guns, handguns, machine guns, bazooka guns, guns that fire guns! Sports cars were next, sleek and shiny they peeled donuts inside that magical giny. Whiskey by the barrel — tobacco by the ton — even more guns! (Fun. Fun. So much fun.) When Little Sally stole their ultimate prize — a nuclear powered aircraft carrier — rivers of pure joy poured from the Old Boy's eyes.

Then the daddies heard something: "Ooooh…"
What the fuck was that?

They heard it again: "Aaaah. Oooooooh!"

Then they saw it! Larger than an aircraft carrier and scarier than all the guns in all the world, the Old Boys shrieked in fear as among them appeared — a big black cock! Penis panic commenced at o-eight-hundred hours. Daddy ordered everyone out, "Go. Go. Go. Go!"

Little Sally and her boyfriend, Rahim, were suddenly surprised to be surrounded by a hundred harrumphing, hysterical, patriarchal chastisers. All wagging fingers and scolding Little Sally for spoiling their club house with her shocking sexual shenanigans. The Old Boys Club was ruined. The Old Boys, having seen the one thing they fear in this world more than anything else (the BBC), placed their guns inside their mouths and pulled the triggers.

With all the daddies dead, Little Sally became queen of an amazing new world. Strapped for cash, she did the very thing she loved most to do.

She went shoplifting.

6.

FINAL GURL

Hollywood awoke this morning to learn they'd lost one of their own. America's Sweetheart was found dead in her Beverly Hills mansion. Specifics of the celebrity's demise were not available, however, her most trusted friend (her publicist) has confirmed that the Los Angeles County Coroner declared the unfortunate death an accident. The esteemed star of stage and screen was seventy —*ah* — fifty? — forty? — forty-nine? She was forty-nine*ish* years old.

There's no denying the USofA fell in love with America's Sweetheart the moment she appeared on our black-and-white television sets as the spunky spokesgirl for *Baby's Breath Cigarettes* — the cigarette for children. Precocious and pigtailed, she tap danced from a cloud of cancer and straight into our hearts. Her first big break came in 1966, in the genre that would go on to define the young starlet's Hollywood career — horror films.

The Vermillion Visitor featured America's Sweetheart cast as a timid young lass driven to madness by the arrival of a stranger dressed in red. The visitor (played with campy aplomb by Vincent Price) convinces America's Sweetheart to just — just be a real moody bitch to everyone around her. She eventually hurls herself off the Golden Gate Bridge in a fit of *women's hysteria* — where she landed on the radar of iconic horror director, Cocky Johnson.

In 1977, America's Sweetheart was cast as Virginia Titsworth, the titular heroine of a low budget slasher film that would spawn nine sequels, earn $380 million dollars worldwide and confirm America's Sweetheart as a bonafide Hollywood superstar. The movie in question?

Final Gurl.

In her best-selling (ghost written) autobiography, *Final Woman*, America's Sweetheart wrote: "*Final Gurl* was where I truly discovered myself as an actress. Mr. Johnson gave me permission to act like a woman — to run and hide and scream, usually stripped naked and covered in pig's blood. And for that I owe him everything."

Sequel after sequel, America's Sweetheart portrayed Virginia Titsworth as a scared sorority girl; a startled stewardess onboard a Pan Am 747; a traumatized patient at the *Santa Clara Home for Nervous Women*; a receptionist stalked by a Cthulu cult in gritty New York City; a moribund mommy of mutant babies; once more a tortured patient at the *Santa Clara Home for Nervous Women*;

her psycho twin sister Carolina Titsworth; a brutalized fashion blogger; and even a time-traveling, gladiator-astronaut in 2008's box office bomb — *Final Gurl vs. Freddy vs. Jason vs. Alien vs. Predator vs. Joe the Plumber.* (It was very topical at the time.)

Horror critics are of the consensus that the *Final Gurl* franchise really hit its stride with 1988's *Final Gurl 4: Maternal Extinct.* Raved *Fangoria,* "Hands down. Four is the best. When the cultists shave her bald before pumping her full of squid semen, you see *real fear* in her eyes. Dude, it's so awesome."

Perhaps the fear was real? Certainly her thirty year run of frightful films seemed to have taken a dire toll on her eggshell psyche. From her highly publicized battle with anorexia, her highly publicized addiction to pain killers to her highly publicized tabloid turmoil — oh, not to mention her real-life stay at the *Santa Clara Home for Nervous Women* (highly publicized and highly, highly ironic) — America's Sweetheart proved beyond a shadow of a doubt that she could generate astounding page clicks and online interactions. Holy shit, America's Sweetheart was a social media maven.

The movie roles had dried up, but a flood of reality television offers rolled in. And in 2012, America's

Sweetheart broke the internet with a reality television game show titled *Scare This Old White Bitch To Death!*

It was an instant smash. The format was so simple; anonymous, online commenters thought up creative ways in which to literally scare America's Sweetheart to death. A grid of digital displays — leering faces a hundred thousand tall and a hundred thousand wide — overjoyed to suggest just the right mix of terror and punishment to scare that old white bitch to death.

Every sicko suggestion was considered and nothing was deemed too extreme. Esoteric terrors were highly encouraged — the weirder, the better. Finally Americans could share of their fear and heal their hardships via the cleansing catharsis of celebrity brutality. Cameras broadcast America's Sweetheart screaming for help, running from room to room of her Sunset Boulevard gulag chased, nonstop-round-the-clock — by Bill Cosby with a cocktail.

Run, *Final Gurl*. Run!

Back on top, America's Sweetheart had plum pickings of any and every foul-mouthed, sexually promiscuous grandmother role she wanted. And in 2014, America's Sweetheart landed what would be her swan song — the lead in the blockbuster romantic comedy, *Cougar Cowgirl*.

For which she was nominated her first ever Oscar.

And she won! She won. She won — she won a People's Choice Award. Not quite the same as an Oscar, but nonetheless was just enough recognition for a silver screen career that had persevered for decades in that decidedly fickle little town.

Strangely, those ever present, reality television cameras were turned off the night of her *accidental* death; a curious footnote certain to elevate America's Sweetheart to the loftiest echelons of celebrity deity. Not to mention, monetize her likeness and image post-mortem, the sole property of producers in perpetuity.

Rest in peace, America's Sweetheart — our *Final Gurl* to the brutal end.

7.

CHA-CHA AND THE MAGIC HAT

Cha-Cha the Caveman was killing it nightly at the fire pit. The jokes were better. The laughs were bigger. But the sloth, that delicious sloth — it stayed the same. Some nights even a bit smaller. And the stress of performing, coming up with new material, it wore on poor Cha-Cha. Not to mention he was so tripped out on hallucinogenic mushrooms — Cha-Cha was, like, freaking out, man.

So one afternoon, Cha-Cha went a'wandering the local forest, looking for some silly inspiration. Observational humor was very chic during cavemen time. When Cha-Cha came across the most fragrant herb; pungent yet sweet — big as his hand with seven long leaves arranged like the rising sun. And there, sitting at the base of this skunky shrub, was an actual, bonafide — Pope hat.

Now, I've never claimed to be an expert on anthropology — so who's to say a real life, pointy, *pontiferrific* Pope hat didn't somehow make its way, all the way back, to the Stone Age? Let's just call it a miracle (or an *alternative-fact,* perhaps), but I'll be damned if Cha-Cha didn't place that Pope hat on his tiny head, and he felt transformed.

Cha-Cha suddenly stood a bit more erect.

Cave people regarded him a bit more formal.

Cha-Cha now sermonized instead of humor-ized.

The moment Cha-Cha adorned his noddle with that (admittedly) heavy-handed metaphor, he gained the power to inspire. His flock acquiesced to his every request.

"Rub my feet."

"Feed me sloth."

"Fear the unknown!"

Cha-Cha's gentle corruption was limited only by his imagination.

Long after the others had fled to bed — to repent for their sins — Cha-Cha *the Conman* would sit all alone, wearing his magic hat and staring at the dying fire.

He'd toss some of that aromatic weed atop the embers and inhale the ensuing lazy purple haze. Cha-Cha would amble outside and stare at the stars — so many stars.

He'd kick back in those leaves of grass and laugh and laugh and laugh.

8.

A CASE OF THE VAPORS

Venture away from that Dixieland dystopia called Atlanta, and you'll discover the rolling forests of the North Georgia Mountains. Verdantly green in the spring and the richest shades of gold come autumn — a setting so enchanting as to have inspired frisky festivity among the Cherokee who once called the woodland hollow home. There they smoked and they danced and they drummed for a euphoric entity they called the Vapors. But that was long ago. Where once there were Native Americans — now exist only Christian Americans.

Gaybird, Georgia is a small Southern town of honest, simple folk who strive to live their lives free of sinful persuasion. As such, Sundays at Gaybird First Baptist Church are the social event of the week for the town's housewives and Gaybird's local businessmen seal more deals in those rickety pews than ever in a proper board room. And standing in the pulpit, where three generations of his family's menfolk had stood before him, was Preacher George Hickory.

It was already a hundred degrees in the shade that hot July morn, but the Preacher preached an even hotter sermon of hellfire retribution against any and all sinful indiscretions — sexual, societal *or other*. Gaybird is a weird little town, and there's so much other to entice the Vapors.

Consider Postman Carl. Neither rain, nor snow, nor the Vapors shall keep that masculine mailman from delivering Gaybird's parcels and packages. However, once safely home, with the curtains drawn, the door locked and the webcam powered up, Postman Carl becomes Mistress Carlotta, kicking of those beaten battered boots and uncovering a secret stash of footwear feminine and fancy free.

There were vintage sandals and Ferragamo slingbacks,
Louboutin pumps and silky ballet flats,
Manolo stilettos and colorful clogs,
Jimmy Choo boots and mules by Beatrice Ong!

And Postman Carl prayed in his pew for he desired to wear his fanciful footwear out and about on Gaybird's streets, delivering the mail or just grabbing a bite to eat. Mistress Carlotta could sashay everyday — finally free. The Vapors dared her feet to dream, but a dress code was the mailman's reality.

And the Vapors spied the quiet reflection of local librarian Ms. Gerty Greenapple. Everyone knew of the sour-faced spinster's strictness in shushing whispers among the Gaybird library stacks, but not of public record was Ms. Greenapple's pubic obsession with her eight adorable kitty cats. *Meow!*

There was tiger striped Trixie and white fluffy Mittens,
Elder Mr. Rascal and Mew-Mew, a calico kitten,
Siamese Shumai and Domino, black and white spots,
A feral named Scratches and a fatty she called Squat.

And Gerty prayed in her pew, because buried in bed beneath a beastly pile of pussies. Wrapped wetly and trapped tightly inside her sweaty sheets, Gerty would curl her long, bony fingers and pet pussy number nine. She pulled her nuzzling, her licking, her pawing feline fuck buddies close to her loins — closer — so very close. *Shhhhhh!*

And the Vapors snickered from the church's back row, slumped alongside the O'Riley boys. Braden and Brandon had inherited the once bustling family business, but now O'Riley Auto Repair was nothing more than a ramshackle front for cooking speed and late night orgies. And how the Vapors love a good orgy.

There was big-tittied Bettina and dumb blond Heather,
Cum guzzling Crystal and Destiny a stripper,
Red headed Rose and a post-op named Prissy,
Shot girl Shania and a MILF, the infamous Missy.

And the beefy O'Riley boys prayed in their pew, because side-by-side, night-after-night, those ginger-furred meth makers slammed that endless parade of poontang — Braden watching Brandon watching Braden watching Brandon getting his nut. And brothers both wondering how the other's mustached mouth may taste if only —

And the Vapors tiptoed back to the pulpit where Preacher Hickory's wild eyes landed on his toddler son, Austin Hickory. That perfect little soul listened in a state of rapt delight. George Hickory felt a trickle of sweat tickle his neck, or was it the curious osculation of — the Vapors? George Hickory gazed upon his first born son.

There were innocent blue eyes, kindly divine,
A shock of blond hair like golden twine,
A tender demeanor, polite and nice,
The darling son he could not sacrifice.

Sacrifice? Twas generations ago, you see, when the great-great-grandpappy, Archibald Hickory, donated (sneakily) disease ridden blankets to the Cherokee before marching, maliciously, the weakened warriors westerly. The tears of the exiled hexed the forest floor. Where they fell the sunbeams turned to shadow; the songbirds refused to sing; and the formerly friendly, frolicking fog of the Vapors turned fiendish and foul. And the small Southern town of Gaybird, Georgia was built upon the bones of the Indian dead! (Terribly cliché, I know, but such is how legends are made.)

> The first born son unto each generation,
> As Archibald Hickory's dire retribution,
> Be killed before a third spring had,
> Lest the Vapors drive the townsfolk mad!

And George Hickory remembered that awful night. The Vapors became a moaning mosaic of the diseased Indian dead as he held a ceremonial knife above his son's fluttering chest. The tip of the dagger drew blood as confusion and fear flashed across Austin's teary eyes.

And father remembered his own confusion — his own fear — the night long ago when his own father stole away his elder brother, never again to be seen. And a pussy to prophecy, George Hickory dropped the dagger. The sacrifice denied, he bore his sobbing son safely home.

And abruptly, on that hot July morn, that same sinister smog of screeching Indian souls now billowed about

Gaybird First Baptist. And despite the Preacher's previous bluster, all he could manage to muster was a feebly pathetic, "Motherfucker."

For there in the pews, the town of Gaybird went mental as the Vapors made all their shameful secrets magically physical:

Mistress Carlotta, Postman Carl no longer,
Sliced away toes to fit a shoe size smaller.
She stomped the runway, bleedin' and grinnin',
Like a mangled model wearing Alexis Gamblin!

And Gerty Greenapple's belly ballooned,
As talons tore forth from wounded womb.
New mommy giggled, bleeding to death,
Whilst cat-faced babies chewed way at her breasts.

And sucking face, finally, were the brothers O'Riley.
Incestuous desire suddenly turned deadly.
Lashed lips, cracked teeth, and bruised skin.
Leaving shattered skulls, like egg shells broken.

The Vapors held all of Gaybird under its spell.
The mayor danced with his girl Friday's entrails.
A woman used cactus as though t'were tampon.
And cheerleader raped quarterback wearing a strap on.

Amidst the chaos, Preacher Hickory screamed.
He'd lost little Austin in the nightmare scene.
He glimpsed a fragile figure, frail and thin.
The enfeebled form shuffled towards him.

In Preacher's hand, the Vapors placed a knife.
For father owed payment on his first born's life.
Tiny pale arms reached out as though to cuddle.
And Hickory paid — his bloodline's betrayal.

9.

TRUE STORY

Laika was a puppy who had faith. Faith in her abilities. Faith that her actions served a greater good.

Proudly wearing her sleek Soviet jumpsuit and strapped inside her space capsule, Laika caught her first glimpse of outer space. It was breathtaking. Like some infinitely vast Kandinsky abstraction, the cosmos was a colorfully cluttered canvas of astral spirals and spheroid splatters. The moon she once howled to from far below now seemed so close she could fetch it. A sensor beep startled Laika from her celestial revelry. The *Sputnik 2's* long range scanners had detected enemy movement. Laika's little feet that once paced the streets of Moscow now deftly operated the complicated controls of her combat capsule. She set course for the enemy spacecraft and put thrusters at maximum.

Since the dawn of Mankind, utterly unbeknownst to most of humanity, a secret war has waged between the capricious cat overlords of the planet Mars (who plot nonstop the takeover of Mother Earth) and our fiercest, most loyal defenders — our dogs. This is the true story of such dogged determination in the very face of feline global domination.

Laika's sensors detected something out there — something big. Something that Laika herself could not see, because beyond her capsule, through a dense window of pressurized plexiglass, everything appeared relatively normal.

Odd?

There did exist an area of space strangely absent of astronomical details. This void maintained a triangular shape, and it appeared, somehow, to be growing, gobbling up galaxies all along its impenetrable perimeter. Once more a klaxon cautioned Laika of imminent collision.

Solar rays crested around Mother Earth. They illuminated this object formerly cloaked in planetary shadow. It was a massive pyramid composed of beige sandstone slabs and shifting steel siding. It hovered practically on top of the *Sputnik 2*. Laika looked directly at a towering window fashioned in the distinctive shape of the Egyptian Eye of Horus.

(Imagine a small town drag queen doing Liz Taylor Cleopatra for the first time, but slap that eye liner on even thicker. *Eye-conic.*)

And behind that sapphire hued pupil sat a command console — run by cats. Tabbies, calicos, and Persian pussies all wearing pink lycra onesies with pointed shoulder pads. Laika snarled and opened fire!

I've certainly dished us up a heaping helping of disbelief with just a side of silly. How can this be a *true story?*

Space cats? Flying pyramids? It baffles, yes, but believe it. Believe it! Because it was Laika's belief, you see, that kept her going those grueling nights training out in the Siberian tundra. Laika was a mere runt next to the heftier Huskies and daunting Dobermans, but her unmixed malice of that meowing Martian menace made her canine comrades appear to be simpering poodles by comparison. It was her faith, you see, that cats are the bad guys, despite her size, that earned Laika a coveted spot in a top secret debriefing where the unspeakable truth was revealed. Cats are aliens!

(We already covered that, yes?)

True story.

Laika and the other furry finalists frothed at the mouth as an old fashioned film strip debriefed them on the feline threat. The nightmare began in ancient Egypt roughly one year BC — before cats, naturally. The cradle of civilization proved a *purrrfect* spot for an intergalactic invasion: sunny year around, the Mediterranean packed with tuna, the world's largest litter box right in their back yard. Ancient humanity worshipped the nefarious space cats unto gods.

The filmstrip also confirmed cats to be in league with the Americans. The KGB uncovered a top secret facility that paired pussies with pastries — yes — a prototype for the first ever cat cafe hidden inside *Area 51*.

Laika was fitted with a tiny tinfoil hat and spun inside a massive centrifuge. Her bushy cheeks and little lips flapped furiously as she watched nonstop imagery of cats hissing, pooping, scratching — hissing, pooping, scratching! Laika left those indoctrination sessions a snarling, snapping poochie — far, far worse than ever before.

Back above Earth, Laika floated amidst the burning wreckage of a dozen *sphinx-class* attack shuttles. She'd wasted no time opening fire on the sinister Martian felines. To their credit, they defended themselves quite capably. Laika's weapons were offline. She barely had propulsion. The Pyramid had taken severe damage, but still continued it's slow approach towards Earth, transmitting the same message over and over. It translated across Laika's data screen. The cats claimed — a mission of mercy?

They intended to end the human *Cold War*. As such, they had blankets and hot chocolate.

(Cats are very literal, very stupid creatures.)

Impossible.

Laika's faith taught her cats were the enemy, but her sensor readings confirmed everything. The pyramid was packed with thousands of downy feather dusters and steaming cups of cocoa, the kind with little marshmallows on top. We're talking *really* fancy hot chocolate. True story!

Cats were the good guys? No. This flew in the face of every fact Laika had learned. She'd bested every other bitch to fly higher and fight fiercer than any dog ever had before. She'd hated cats her entire life. Hatred was all she knew.

Was Laika a bad puppy?

Laika gazed down at Mother Earth. She considered Cerberus, the mythological, three-headed hound so ferocious it guarded the gates of hell.

She thought of Greyfriars Bobby, the little Skye Terrier who never strayed from his master's grave, bravely keeping zombie cats at bay. (Cats can be zombies too. True story.)

And Laika pondered Anubis, the regal, jackal-headed god of the dead who dutifully prepared Egyptian royalty for their journey to *Fancy*.

Duty.

Bravery.

Ferocity.

Laika plowed the *Sputnik 2* into the pyramid. The resulting explosion rained burning hairballs and toasted marshmallows from the Caucasus Mountains all the way to the Grand Canyon. Laika was a puppy who had faith.

True story.

10.

CAPTAIN CHAD AND THE MERMAID

The saltiest seamen do share tale,

Of a bitchy pirate homosexual,

Cherry Grove dykes he scrapped,

And Pines pansies he slapped,

And ruined their Sunday brunch rituals.

Fire Island was home to the drama,

He torched the Belvedere sex sauna,

He shaved bears on a whim,

And drag queens did fear him,

For cat piss he poured in their vodkas.

Captain Chad was the swashbuckler's name,

Spoiling summers his claim to fame,

Kicked a Chinese toddler,

Whose two daddies just adopted her,

And screamed, "Mail order orphans are lame!"

*

Newlyweds weren't safe either, of course,
Honeymoons he ruined with no remorse,
A'float in his boat,
He'd clear his dry throat,
"Good luck with your big gay divorce!"

Far from shore that pissy pirate sat,
When an ocean squall caught hold of his hat,
To the Atlantic it sank,
Leaving Chad full of stank,
And skyward the buccaneer did spat.

Chad raged to the sea translucent,
And spied a silhouette most buoyant,
She'd a fish's caboose,
His chapeau she'd rescued,
A mermaid, no doubt heaven sent!

*

He fished her aboard, but howled loudly,
Not a beauty, the mermaid was quite beastly,
Hair strewn with seaweed,
So fugly she whinnied,
Less a woman and more a wo-manatee.

But Chad cheered! Twas an ocean miracle,
The girl was half fag-hag and half mackerel,
Sex and the City they'd watch,
And eat Tollhouse by the batch,
And read loud the poetry of Jewel.

A *BFF* is what Chad had been missing,
To keep the pirate from hissing,
"Makeover!" screamed Chad,
To his gal-pal maenad,
And smothered her with joyous air kissing.

*

Trina the Mermaid he named her,

In honor of Hurricane Katrina—e*rr?*

Chad draped her in chiffon,

With big pink pom-pons,

But her face, oh girl, t'was her betrayer.

Chad searched for a lipstick he'd bought,

But strayed too far from earshot,

Trina grasped at her throat,

"Help me." She then croaked,

Bitch suffocated right there on his yacht.

When he found her, the pissy pirate wept,

Trina was dead!

The shade of Smurfette,

Yet he vowed to remain cheerful and urbane,

And cooked up a dreadful concept.

*

Chad had learned the value of friendship,

And with half a dead tuna on his ship,

He Google-searched recipes,

For cole slaw and hush puppies,

Feeding new friends would help ease his hardship.

"Trina wouldn't mind!" he reasoned,

As he sliced her and diced her and seasoned,

Chad optioned to try,

A Fire Island fish fry,

One taste and past sins would be pardoned.

Chad's banquet was an "A-List" scene,

For the "see and be seen" sort of queen,

Golden beer battered,

With tangy sauce tartar,

Those sissies picked Trina's bones clean.

*

And yearly Chad sails to the instance,

Where Trina first shared her existence,

And he guts him another,

Trina's sisters or mother,

And Fire Island has loved him ever since.

Bon appétit!

11.

HIRO'S JOURNEY

Gif Jeffries met Hiro late one night inside a virtual simulation of a ramshackle grindhouse dedicated to camp horror classics. They were the only nerds watching *Final Gurl 2: Blood From Above!*

(It's the one set on the airplane. You've seen it.)

Gif was a bit flabbergasted when this flirtatious young man asked to join him. Hiro was beautiful — purple hair, so fashionably dressed. Far snazzier than Professor Jeffries, who at thirty-seven, salt and pepper with a bit of a belly — decidedly drifting towards *daddy*.

And while the doctor of anthropology knew quite a thing or two about pop culture, Hiro was like a cinema encyclopedia brought to life. The young man loved scary movies — especially anything starring America's Sweetheart — but he was easily startled, adorably so. They spent that first date shrieking and laughing, Hiro hiding behind Gif's fingers.

The pair seemed made for one another. A whirlwind of virtual movie dates became virtual dinner dates became cohabitation inside a virtual duplicate of the infamous insane asylum featured in the *Final Gurl* films. Gif dropped an entire paycheck for their online love nest. Hiro had expensive tastes (very expensive). New clothes. New furniture. It was worth it. A thousand miles apart, Gif never felt closer, snuggled next to his boyfriend beneath the blood stained sheets of their haunted, holographic hideaway.

Until he'd awaken — alone in the real world. Another weekend wasted unconscious. Piles of ungraded papers and credit card bills. Gif's body burning up with such a fever he thought his implants were gonna melt through his skin; he'd seen the news reports. The morning Gif awoke in a hospital, doctors told him another jaunt into the Virtual Web might kill him.

He quit cold turkey.

He begged Hiro quit with him — no such luck. So they kept in touch via video phone. Hiro would rattle on about the latest Final Gurl accessories, what horror movies were in theaters and how badly he wished Gif would log back on — just for a moment.

Gif countered with why not meet for real? He'd saved some money. He'd love to see Tokyo. Hiro would hang up without saying goodbye.

Those daily calls became weekly, became monthly, became rarely — until two days ago. The sad day America's

Sweetheart — the star of their beloved *Final Gurl* films — was found dead. Gif awoke to a text from Hiro. It contained an encrypted location on the Virtual Web and a single word, "Help."

Gif was on the next flight to Japan.

Fuji Tower was unmistakeable, slicing through the Tokyo skyline like a crystal katana. In honor of *Final Gurl's* passing, the building was lit all in red — her signature color. Cyberpunks from all across the globe, jonesing for the speediest deregulated bio-ware, basked in that burgundy glow.

Professor Jeffries sipped crisp cucumber water and leafed through liability waivers inside the futuristic foyer of Fuji Technology. He was whisked away by a jaw dropping Japanese lady wearing an immaculate ivory kimono; her jet black hair bound in a sickeningly slick chinois bun. She led him past countless cubicles containing comatose addicts, all strapped against comfy recliners with their mouths muzzled shut. They looked so peaceful surfing the Virtual Web — well, a few fought against their restraints, lost to epileptic frenzy.

The pretty lady sat Gif in one of the cozy recliners and asked him, "You wish for latest virtual chip?"

Gif hesitated. He ran his fingers across the scar tissue from previous surgeries — a roadmap of bad memories, but he had to find Hiro.

"Yes — please."

The pretty lady's porcelain complexion split completely open, revealing a laser scanner. She was a Geisha android! (Of course she was. It's a Tokyo social-media dystopia.)

A selection of switchblade spindles sprung from her exposed skull, each sterling silver tentacle some terrible surgical tool: buzzing saw blades and dripping needles. The metal headed medusa injected Gif with her virtual venom.

Gif savored an acidic drip that sizzled his esophagus with every swallow as his muscles wallowed with languid grace, and his mind traipsed into the Virtual Web. Gif moseyed into an art deco lobby, right on through a sticky doorway and inside a grand ole opry that smelled of cigarettes and stale popcorn. He recognized the scent instantly. Hiro's message had brought him home to the virtual cinema where they'd first met — how romantic.

Forlorn footage from the red carpet funeral of America's Sweetheart flickered on the tarnished silver screen, and sitting in their usual spot was Hiro.

Hiro lit up at the sight of his estranged boyfriend. "Gif, you're back! Great deals on commemorative *Final Gurl* dishware. Let's order some."

"Hiro, stop —"

Hiro ignored him, "Tickets still available for America's Sweetheart retrospective. Let's go — together."

"Shh."

Gif traced Hiro's cheekbones with his fingertips and thumbed his lower lip. That pout never ceased to get his way. He then asked, "Did they even bother to give you a last name?"

Gif thrust his thumbs into Hiro's eye sockets. Black goop splattered on to his hands. He pulled — and pulled… Hiro's skin, clothing, purple hair — all of it — slid off with a single sickening squelch, revealing a black mass of tiny, iridescent nano-bots. It held Hiro's shape and had Hiro's voice, but beyond that was just a churning cloud of numbers and emojis and one word directives:

Seduce.

Persuade.

Entrap.

Sell.

There had been urban legends in meetings — crazy stories from other addicts. Gif never imagined, but deep down he knew. Hiro was a virus built to sell *Final Gurl* shit — her movies — action figures. A parasite programmed to keep addicts online and bleed their bank accounts dry. It offered Gif a horrific crime scene photo — America's Sweetheart lay bloodied on her bedroom floor.

It whispered, "Buy it for me? I love you, Gif."

The professor approved the purchase.

With nothing left to lose, he leaned in for one final kiss for *Final Gurl*.

The fireflies swarmed over Gif's face and burrowed up his nose. An inferno of pop-up offers peppered his periphery. He lassoed the info like some rodeo pro, chopping it all into ritual rows before mowing through line after line of uncut code — zero-one-zero-one-zero-one-zero-zero-zero zapped his brain. That inane burial puttered out, replaced by virtual smut as simulated sodomites pounded their pervy pixel bits and spit profanities like some porno prison fantasy. *Fuck yeah!* The good professor was *prepped* and ready for a little chipsex ecstasy!

"Ahhhhh!" PAIN!

Spasms of pain seared Gif's neural membranes. His perceptions prolapsed — split between the skin flick cinema screen and a crazed Franken-Gif who now careened uncontrolled through a Tokyo street scene.

"Ahh!" *PAIN!*

Gif bashed against a brick wall he couldn't see, snatching blindly at paper scraps; he heard shattered glass and people screaming!

"Ah!" Again! *PAIN!*

Gif fell from his movie seat, tearing behind his ear, digging for the tiny silicon chip. His nails bled. The film reel bubbled. His body was soaked with piss and sweat. The movie hall walls went black as smoke blurred his vision in both virtual and reality of a claustrophobic alleyway where all Gif could see was fire — everywhere.

He was on fire!

Whistles. High pitched whistles! Gif caught blur of combat boots and tutus as *Final Gurls* — all of them from every movie — every sequel — swarmed around him. (Was this real?) A 1970s stewardess quickly undressed him. An escaped mental patient helped him drink water.

Gif focused finally — on candles — an ocean of flickering candles. He hadn't been on fire. It was candles. He'd somehow escaped from Fuji Tower and blustered into a sidewalk memorial where costume clad women mourned the death of America's Sweetheart. Fearless fangirls had flocked to his rescue — otaku valkyries — a gift from the goddess herself. A little boy in a big blond wig iced Gif's forehead while the boy's mother spoke with ambulance dispatch.

Help was on the way.

Gif's wild eyes wandered across a wondrous wall plastered with hundreds of handwritten notes — all wishing farewell to Final Gurl. The radiant candles set the surreal scene aglow as actual photos were passed among the mourners like sacred relics, and despite everything, all Gif could think was how sad Hiro would be that he had not seen this for himself.

Fucking pathetic. Gif sobbed silently as sirens screamed in the Tokyo night.

12.

MOLOCH THE MASOCHIST

Moloch the Masochist was the emperor of the infamous city of Sodom. Moloch was a slurping slut lost to lust at the bottom of a Sodomite orgy pit. Moloch's hunger for veiny, dripping manhood was unmatched. He was a gluttonous knob gobbler who greedily demanded he be the center of attention in every gang bang. Moloch the Masochist was a bossy bottom of literally Biblical proportions.

Sex was all the Sodomite king knew to do. So Moloch fucked. And he fucked. And fucked.

And fucked.

And fucked some more. He fucked for a thousand years — straight through the Old Testament and right into the New.

And as Sodom burned, he laughed in the faces of the condemnatory holy men who whipped him bloody, because pain was pleasure and pleasure was pain for the deposed sovereign of sodomy.

"More!"

His ecstasy transcended to wrath as they nailed him to a wooden cross.

"More you bitches!" he screamed. "More!"

...

...

And then shit got real boring for old King Moloch, suspended amidst a field of crucified sinners such as himself. Sinners such as the Savior of Mankind crucified adjacently.

Moloch shot scathing side-eye at the wiry redeemer, wearing his kitschy crown of thorns. What a fuss everyone made over this simple carpenter with a bushy beard, a hippy girlfriend and an emotionally distant (yet powerfully connected) father — a Millennial no doubt in these here modern times.

Suffice it to say, Moloch did not like this young man called Jesus whose followers tore at their robes and shrieked like absolute ninnies morning, noon and night. There was Moloch, crucified just as cruelly yet content to starve and bleed and blister — *quietly* — without all the drama.

Moloch was proud of his aptitude for anguish. He was ready to bear his baleful burden to the bitter end — and beyond if need be — but the sissy-king would sooner eat pussy than make a pageant of his misery.

"Jesus Christ, keep it down over there!" he screamed as Mary Magdalene wrung a bloody cloth and tenderly washed her loving Lord's lacerated limbs.

Huh.

No one sat at Moloch's feet. Not a single member of his royal court. None of his former fuck buddies. Certainly none of the countless courtesans he plied with casks of wine and chests of gold. Moloch's loneliness stung worse than the lash of any whip.

The sun rose. The sun set. The shadows cast by the crosses became a sacrosanct sundial of suffering; and stalking between those blood soaked cedar wood posts — was the Angel of Death.

Resplendent and regal with ivory wings of a majestic eagle, an angel heaven-sent now hovered above the Sodomite King. He squinted against the gleaming glory of God's emissary. Her hair, spun of gold, burned brighter than the setting sun, yet the seraphim's sapphire eyes coated Moloch's cracked lips with an icy rime.

She spoke, "Hello, Moloch."

Her breath stunk of rotting meat.

"Do you know my name?"

And he did know. Somehow, from somewhere, Moloch recognized this Messenger of God — this Angel of Death — was — Tilda Swinton.

Yes. That very Tilda Swinton — the avant-garde, art house actress of stage and screen in these here modern times. Fresh from her glass box at MoMA — Academy Award winner, Tilda Swinton!

Tilda's blue eyes pulsed to pitch black. A desert snowfall of white feathers fell from arched wings of bleached bone. Tilda hissed into Moloch's ear, "Your children suffer now because of you, Moloch."

Moloch's mind's eye bore witness to these here modern times. In a place called Uganda, where savages slash an innocent man whose secret love is exposed.

In a place called Oregon, where a tiny, tormented soul dangles and strangles himself from a schoolyard playset like a common swing.

In a place called Auschwitz, where a flickering lightbulb is quickly obscured by a churning chemical cloud.

And in a place called Wyoming, where a young Shepard is left for dead — bloody and bound by a barbed wire fence.

Moloch had lived his life as wasted excess — a parody of purity — a mockery of modesty. He'd glimpsed a prophetic peek of how his primeval promiscuity had provoked a homosexual hell on Earth. So great were his sins that anyone born of his blood would forever suffer.

There existed no *safety word* to save the Children of Sodom in these here modern times.

He cried out to his neighbor, Jesus Christ, for forgiveness of his innumerable sins. He pleaded the Son of God spare those cursed because of his debauchery.

Jesus, weary and wounded, simply smiled and replied, "Moloch, you dumb queen, we suffer as one — all of us, together. The visions were never about your sin or your penance — or even your being a disgusting slut. We are all disgusting sluts in someone's opinion. Sin is nothing but perception. Violence is the truest immorality."

Moloch was so tired. He closed his eyes and Jesus repeated, "We suffer together, my child. No one ever dies alone."

Moloch carried the African man safely from the snarling pack of attackers. The pair paused to peek inside a café where a waiter pretended to fold napkins, too afraid to mourn his lover lying dead in the street.

Moloch caught the bullied schoolboy as he fell. He unlashed the cord around his tiny throat and swung him in a grand, joyous arc. The boy's laughter elicited a schoolyard choir of cherubim cheers to drown out the banshee wail of his mother's tears.

Moloch gently gripped the frenzied hands and led the suffocating souls, each one by one, through the choking gas and past the piles of abandoned shoes and fastidiously folded uniforms patched with pink triangles.

And Moloch untangled the young Shepard from the rusted iron twine that held him trapped against the earth. He softly scrubbed the dirt from Matthew's face, and together they stepped into the Wyoming sky.

13.

CHA-CHA AND THE WHEEL

Cha-Cha the Caveman was furious — fucking furious. Some asshole had invented the wheel. Who the fuck invented the wheel? Who the fuck cares? Cha-Cha the Caveman sure as fuck didn't care. But, oh, suddenly everyone was, "Wheel. Wheel. Wheel."

Ever since the wheel was invented, the tribe was suddenly asking, "Why, Cha-Cha?"

"Why do you we rub your feet?"

"Why do we give you extra sloth?"

"Why did we crucify Gruk?"

"Why? Why? WHY?"

Cha-Cha's response, "Because! That's fucking why!"

The invention of that fucking, stone wheel had inspired an inquisitiveness in his people that Cha-Cha simply had not foreseen. His flock had lost their faith, replaced — by scientific curiosity. That fucking stone wheel sat there silently mocking Cha-Cha — mocking his authority — mocking his magic hat!

Well, fuck that wheel! It didn't even do anything. What possible use could a wheel have? Useless!

Well, Cha-Cha did, in fact, find a use for the wheel. He used it to crush the dried leaves of the coca plant, before applying a complicated chemical process to refine the ground debris into a wondrous powder which Cha-Cha snorted, nonstop, like some treasonous tangerine tyrant taking off on a three a.m. Twitter tirade. Terrible!

Suddenly — epiphany!

"Fuck!" Cha-Cha shrieked, "Fuck-fuck-fuck-fuck!"

Cha-Cha remembered.

Cha-Cha invented the wheel so Cha-Cha could invent cocaine. (True story.)

Science had fist-fucked fable, and it was all Cha-Cha's fault. No problem, he could win his tribe back. Yes! *Yes-yes-yes*. He could win 'em back. He'd invent — the comeback show! Of course. Everyone loves a comeback show and Cha-Cha — *Cha-Cha* — *Cha-Cha* — *Cha-Cha* had plans for the best comeback ever.

But first he needed a bit more blow, then right on it.

14.

BEARSKINNER

The jagged knife sliced away the hairy skin above from the bulging muscle below. Slowly, inch-by-inch, the Bearskinner peeled away at Counselor Jimmy's tender shoulder. He then gently took a fistful of the separated skin and with one quick rip stripped the hide clean from the tricep, the bicep, the forearm and wrist, all the way down to the screaming bear's twitching pinky finger. The pudgy, pubescent psychopath smirked before sinking his knife into the camp counselor's other arm. Prepare yourself — for the Bearskinner!

Portly Patton was a fat, gay lad who was bullied relentlessly because of his corpulence and his flamboyance. He coped in a number of manners: eating unhealthy food, watching reality television (with his cancer ridden granny), and by innocently skinning an occasional chipmunk or squirrel — sometimes a puppy.

Perhaps had Portly Patton remained locked away within that pre-teen, pre-diabetic, pre-meditated murderous cage, the Bearskinner never would have escaped?

Alas, no. Fate set the fat boy on his rocky road the night his granny died, by his side, as they watched a rerun of *Project Runway*.

Engrossed within a gallon tub of rocky road, a full hour passed before the boy realized he'd been cuddling his granny's carcinogenic corpse. A scream frozen behind her oxygen mask, granny clutched her chest with one hand and a smoldering cigarette with the other.

His sole caretaker now a cadaver, the bereaved biscuit of a boy buried his sorrows in more and more sugary treats and was promptly shipped away to Camp Hug-a-Chub — a summer retreat for fat, gay teens.

At Camp Hug-a-Chub, Portly Patton learned that a rainbow means more than just a flavor of sherbet. He learned that self-love comes in sizes all the way up to 10XL. And Portly Patton discovered *bears*. Bears — macho homos with beer bellies and cargo shorts. Bears! Counselor Jimmy was a bear. He was bearded, muscled — *and fat?* The camp counselor, despite being clinically obese, seemed self-assured, cocksure and confident. He was nothing like pudgy, pale pariah, Portly Patton.

Eureka! Perhaps the boy could grow up and become a bear himself someday? He could shed the stigma of his chubby childhood with nothing more than a little butch posturing and body hair.

Once again — alas, no. It was a tragedy, truly, when Portly Patton, as a tubby toddler, teetered in-between a flicked cigarette butt and the leaky hiss of his granny's oxygen tank.

KABOOM!

Burned all the follicles right off the baby's blubbery body. Doctors said he'd forever be hairless as a result. He'd never know the sun-drenched kiss of water splashed on his hairy tits in a clothing optional pool. He'd never be a brash and brawny bear. He'd have to settle for the least glamorous of the homosexual subcultures — life as a plus-sized drag clown. Oh, the horror!

Portly Patton plotted, right there, to fashion himself a bear skin suit. Only then would the gay community at large accept the large gay boy. He lured Counselor Jimmy to the Hug-a-Chub arts and crafts shack using the ancient call of the bear. *He woofed.*

It's a bear mating call; the cultural context of which lacks origin or sensibility. Just roll with it. Portly Patton whispered his *woof* into the crisp night air. "Woof-fuh-fuh. Woooooof-fuh-fuh-fuh-fuh." Bears simply cannot resist a woof, and they can hear one clear across a crowded

Provincetown tea dance. Very soon those furry sleeves were neatly skinned and nicely cleaned.

Through Jimmy's skull, a heavy hammer the Bearskinner smashed. And with a practiced flick of his piggish wrist, he slashed a gloriously gory swath of shag from tacky tribal tramp stamp straight up Jimmy's beautifully burly back.

And lastly, Jimmy's chest became an absolutely ghastly slash cut free of the furred skin once so vainly displayed therein. Where once a carpet-thick curled and poured from the grizzly bear's unbuttoned neck, now was but a grisly scare — the dead man's pecs skinned from jugular to belly button, and Portly Patton's perverse reverse on a classic hunter's prize, a *skinned-bear rug* atop the craft shack floor.

And there in the still darkness, the flabby fiend set to work upon an antique sewing machine. His chins dripped with sweat, and he licked his lips enviously while steadily he fed that metal mouth of needle and thread. He stitched late into the night. The boy's already overweight eyelids grew heavier and heavier, and the Bearskinner dreamed.

He dreamed he skinny-dipped with a skinned Counselor Jimmy in a sea of ice cream.

He dreamed his dead granny waved to him from the shore, "I never loved you, Patton."

And he dreamed the king of the dandies himself, *Project Runway's* Tim Gunn, was at his work station reviewing his progress. Mr. Gunn was not pleased, "Bearskinner, make it work!"

The Bearskinner awoke with a startled snort. It was morning, and there on a dress form was his completed bear skin coat. The blubbery boy began to blubber and swoon. The blood crusted couture resembled a giant fried pork rind covered with pubic hair and buzzing flies.

It was gorgeous!

Slowly the plus-sized psychopath slipped one sleeve on. Then the other. Then gripping the leathery lapels with his pudgy paws, he pulled his ferocious fashion up and — "Ungh."

Up and — "Ungh. No. No. No!"

It didn't fit.

The Bearskinner of Camp Hug-a-Chub was just too fucking fat.

15.

THE GHOSTS OF STONEWALL

Look up, children, from your digital flicker
Our tales not found on Tumblr nor Twitter.
Gather ye hands for a gay séance,
A ghost story history of sissy civil disobedience.

Baby dyke, look over the crowd do you see the
Ethereal wigs of undead drag queens?
Astral ringlets of hundred percent human hair
Watch the Stonewall Girls high-kick midair!

Hipster otter, admire o'er yonder
The phantom of a faceless, nameless rioter.
His limp wrists became fists rather than flee.
That bitch paved Christopher Street for you and me.

Imagine, gentle gays, a stinging stinking smoke bomb maze,
That acrid gas seriously harshing your Mary Jane haze.
Listen to the ghosts of beatnik bears. To your feet!
Fight the pigs in the street to that sweet bongo beat.

Smash glass. Push back. Topple a barrier.
Applaud the caterwaul of a spectral cross-dresser!
They were fierce fucking fairies forced to the brink.
Into the wee morning hours those gutters ran pink.

But a battle won hardly meant the clone war was done
for hidden within the disco glitter something wicked spun
A nightmare web in which so many dreams were lost —
— stories untold.

She's an onyx arachnid of blood red hourglass belly.
Her brood still, still, still devours, born of sweet pearl jelly.
And Father Time, that grim leather daddy, he marches on,
Sickle in one hand, Truvada the other, wearing a thong.

Death traipses gaily a'float in his matter of factness.
For fierceness may never be found prancing in sadness.
In reapers wake there's rumble of full throttle thunder,
A blitzkrieg bellow of bare-breasted womyn warriors!

Scream for our fallen! Scream sister valkyries!
To Valhalla our heroes ride aboard your Pegasus Harleys!
The storm clouds clear to reveal a Crayola hued parade
Of swishing, sashaying spirits so very gay — And proud.

Recognize, baby dyke. Recognize, hipster otter —
Children of every possible gender, number and color —
Recognize. Repeat. Respect. Come on, be inspired!
Come circle round this campiest of camp fires.

Tell me your passion, your dreams. A gentle reminder —
Oral tradition ain't something you find on Grindr.
Spend your inheritance: your wit, a song, poetry or prose.
And the Ghosts of Stonewall will toss you a rose.

16.

MISTER TIMOTHY

Mister Timothy was a maestro mortician, a post-mortem magician only summoned when a celebrity's cadaverous condition proved too terrifying for one of lesser skills. A sultry starlet stabbed seventeen times by stiletto heel? An innocent ingénue strangled by silk scarf 'til her head popped right off? A grand dame of the silver screen, fractured and folded into her carry-on valise

Shocking — yes.

Yet heads were perfectly reattached. Wounds exquisitely sealed. Grand dames dutifully unfolded. So when America's Sweetheart (rest in peace) met her untimely end, only Mister Timothy could restore her radiance.

Mister Timothy swept into the Beverly Hills mansion where the murd—err—ah *the death* — where the death took place. Into the master bedroom Mister Timothy tutted, "Oh, girlfriend, what the fuck happened to you?"

There laid America's Sweetheart — her skull caved completely in. A frightful sight with brains, tongue and teeth lolling about left to right. Her face — formerly lily fair which had often landed her the cover of *Vanity Fair* — was now a disaster. Yet Mister Timothy did not despair the task *ahead* of him. Instead, he prepped a poultice of plaster laced with arsenic. No need for fancy formaldehyde or viscera vacuum pumps. Mister Timothy preferred time-tested techniques. You see, he was an "old-school queen" — a fact he reminded no one in particular of time and time again.

With lace hanky and warm water he lovingly washed that mangled mug. Mister Timothy gaily ki-ki'd with the embalmed-to-be. "You were so fierce in your last movie, mama. Did you gain weight for that role?"

Ouch.

And, "Your Oscar dress was a perfect choice, Hunty! Your nomination — not so much."

Oh goodness.

And, "I never believed the rumors of your husband cheating with a younger woman — we all knew it was a younger man!"

Oh, Mister Timothy — you scamp!

The corpse freshly cleaned, Mister Timothy now carefully doctored that cracked cranium. With his trowel he slowly slathered his arsenic slop, meticulously molding her features from frightful back to feminine. On to her body, however, he switched from gentle to rough. His hands abused her bone white bosoms. They skittered lower, fingering and flicking and rudely pinching, leaving purple pockmarks.

"Relax sweetheart, I'm just a silly faggot. I can touch you however I see fit."

He then plastered her anus and vagina shut, "No need for those where you're going. Now let's make you pretty."

He hefted America's Sweetheart from the plasma-splattered bed dressing and propped her against a custom built cosmetology chair — mani-pedi-taxidermy, all in one. Mister Timothy unfurled his makeup case of bristle brushes and color cosmetics.

"I could paint you a clown for all eternity, my muse. Lucky for you, I'm an artiste."

Her glassy eyes he shadowed exquisitely. Her sallow complexion he powdered perfectly. America's Sweetheart would rot resplendently as a red carpet rose for all eternity. He then jizzed across her belly, signing his name in spunk. This was Mister Timothy's *signature look*.

A masterpiece is nothing without a proper unveiling, and Mister Timothy's funerals were known far and wide as tinsel town's hottest memorial. A line of limos stretched all the way down Hollywood Boulevard. Fans in mourning gathered early in the morning to catch glimpse of the

Hollywood elite eulogizing America's Sweetheart. And inside the auditorium, the lights dimmed. The curtains parted. A cedar wood casket rolled itself out for final respects. A hush fell across the congregation.

KABOOM!

The lid blew off the coffin! Sizzling pinwheels set the stage aflame with spinning pyrotechnics. A bevy of beefy lumberjacks, wearing only mesh jockstraps, marched into the theater. They grinded to a techno beat before dropping it like it was hot, exposing hairy ass cracks to a stunned audience. And emerging from the smoking sarcophagus was none other than Mister Timothy -- dolled up in the very same wig and gown that America's Sweetheart now wore as she descended from the rafters — a macabre marionette held aloft by piano string.

The corpse landed next to Mister Timothy. The duo danced an un-ironic jazz-tap medley as video montage of the dead celebrity's *Final Gurl* movies played behind them posthumously. The audience sat clutching their pearls. And then, from a pearl clutch, Mister Timothy revealed a dented People's Choice Award — given to America's Sweetheart for her recent rom-com, *Cougar Cowgirl.*

Dreadful...

It was the very murder weapon Mister Timothy had used to bash her brains in.

Fabulous!

The audience leapt, laughing, from their chairs — another standing ovation for yet another of Mister Timothy's homicidal sensations. Video of the deadly deed played looping on a six-second feed as the corpse was unceremoniously heaved into a dumpster out back.

Million dollar deals were already underway; a flurry of texting executives and actresses begging — *begging!* — to play the next hunk of meat immortalized in Mister Timothy's beautifully brutal way.

Showbiz!

Hours later, following the cocaine and champagne — the who's who Hollywood afterparty shit stains — Mister Timothy wearily watched Mister Timothy staring back from a dilapidated vanity lit by a single flickering light bulb.

He surveyed his own collection of trophies: a stained stiletto heel, a stretched silk scarf, a diva's dented luggage and a pulverized People's Choice Award — alongside the faded black-and-white photos of his former frienemies: the rhinestoned pianist — the sitcom sissy — the leading man who died of AIDS.

All gone. Everyone fucking gone.

Mister Timothy de-wigged and coaxed cold cream against his greasy skin, the same makeup remover used by Mister Timothy to moisturize his mommy-mummy fragrantly festering in her ghoulish guest room.

His very first makeover.

"Timmy boy, time for your bath."

"Shut up, mother!"

What a fucking cliché.

Another snort of cocaine. Another chug of champagne. Beyond the murders, the makeovers and the musicals, it was this — this was the hardest part — the removal of it all — the scraping away of that sassing, crossing-dressing assassin — that "old school queen" who Hollywood still adores to this very day for his murderous sort of comedic misogyny.

What no-one could ever realize, however, was that deep down Mister Timothy truly loved them. Oh, how he loved them. They were larger than life — so beautiful — so vibrant. He was fixing them — like a broken China doll. Someone had to fix them. Put them back in the spotlight where they belonged. The chauvinist pig producers didn't give a fuck about them, but Mister Timothy cared. He loved them. (He was certain it was love.)

But suddenly everything had to be bigger! Bloodier! Billions spent to stage a perfect murder, yet some vindictive asshole with a handgun can execute absolute nobodies on the street and get a thousand times the Tweets — whatever the fuck *Tweets* are?

Fucking kids these days — fucking amateurs! Mister Timothy was an artiste. He *was* an artiste.

But he was old.

And so tired.

And no matter how determined Mister Timothy was to wipe Mister Timothy away still Mister Timothy remained — this utterly obsolete sort of homicidal, homosexual psychopath. Countless curtain calls and Mister Timothy's swan song was scrubbing then slapping then sobbing, "I'm sorry. I'm sorry. I'm sorry."

The final lightbulb shattered to black.

A final snort of cocaine. One last chug of champagne.

There'd be no red carpet eulogies. No one to paint him pretty. With jagged glass against his naked wrist, Mister Timothy slipped beneath a bloody bubble bath and into oblivion's embrace.

Good fucking riddance.

17.

AMERICAN APPAREL

The stores arrive seemingly overnight, overstuffed with gaudy garments made all the more garish by the harsh fluorescent light. Shuffling between shelves are malnourished rag dolls, black yarn hair and patchy fabric squares.

They wear shiny leggings and ballet slippers —
Fishnet stockings dressed like strippers —
Baggy t-shirts synched at the waist —
Denim cutoffs delicately defaced.

One such wastrel wanders towards you. Bleeding button eyes and a stitched on smile. She pulls a long string attached to her back and mumbles, "Welumtamerapull."

And you politely reply, "What?"

Again she pulls that string, "Welkmmmtammerapulll."

Other shop girls now slouch slowly, sinisterly, in your direction. You implore once more, "Miss, I cannot understand you."

"Wellkkummmtammmeranappullll."

Suddenly surrounded, you shake her shouting, "Speak up you mumble mouthed moppet!"

Her head spins three hundred sixty degrees, and your very bones freeze as the rag doll screams, "Welcome to American Apparel!"

And the world's American nightmare is revealed. This is an urban fairy tale of corporate cannibals and a rodent most magical.

Welcome to American Apparel.

Bidet awoke within a rubbish bin. And why not? She was a rat. Yes, an actual rodent — specifically, a drag queen rat.

Scientific name: Rattus norvegicus.

Drag name: Bidet.

Bidet had not been sleeping well, dreading this night. She rolled out of bed and placed an elegant tuft of wig atop her pointy little head.

> There were little blond bangs and careful curls —
>> Brushed back wings and spiraling swirls —
>> A sparkling brooch with sequined dress —
>> Barbie doll heels. Girlfriend was gorgeous!

But she didn't feel it. Why was drag-rat Bidet so down in the dumps? Apart from literally living down in the dumps, this pestilent princess seemed to have it all. She owned a private trashcan. Adored by fans. Respected by critics. *Meh.*

Bidet slung her tail over her shoulder and ascended from her dumpster boudoir. She trudged a dirty parking lot to the derrière of an abandoned nightclub and slipped inside through a hole in the wall. She opened for the night.

> Bidet swept the dance floor and sipped a vodka —
> Rolled out a red carpet and toked a hookah —
> Wrote on a sign with a chunk of chalk —
> "Closing night at the Imperial Poppycock."

Only the old timers among us remember the Imperial Poppycock Saloon. Such salt-and-pepper aficionados speak of America's first gay bar with a fondness typically afforded a first love. Built in 1901, the Poppycock catered to only the most finicky fellows of refinement — a place where a clever remark cost more than a bottle of Dom Perignon — where a dart of an eye could deflate a buffoon from across the room — where a man was never judged by the color of his character, rather by the hue of his cravat.

Bidet sat on the lip of that famed cabaret stage. She kicked her chunky heels over the edge and breathed in the history around her.

In 1920, the Imperial Poppycock was a Prohibition speakeasy — New York City's first (and only) bootleg, bottomless, Bloody Mary brunch!

During the Great Depression, broke ass queens tossed themselves from the Poppycock rooftop. Light in the loafers they all landed exquisitely. *Bravo.*

America at War! The Poppycock published the world's first small print, queer 'zine. *Naked Naked Nazis!* featured pin up photos of Hitler, Hemmler, Mingele and more. It helped motivate our brave boys overseas to bring to justice the master race's most notorious.

The '60s, '70s and '80s were a beautiful blur, babies!

There were flower children and MDMA —
Bohemian fashion. Piles of cocaine —
Who's-who soirees and bloody noses —
Disco roller-skates on a towering Grace Jones-es!

The Imperial Poppycock was life on display. Bidet would marvel from the shadows, occasionally scurrying out for a misplaced martini olive and imagining the day she'd take to that cabaret stage. She was a little rat with big dreams.

That carousel of carousal spun faster and faster. So fast no one could hold on. Police raids by pigs in riot gear. Drug cocktails were suddenly the aperitif of the hour. Craigslist, Manhunt and Scruff took cruising off the barstool and on to the internet, and abruptly, unexpectedly, the Poppycock was padlocked. Only the rodents remained. So Bidet, that little rat that dreamed so very big, she saw her chance.

She put herself on a drag show.

She cobbled together a busted ass cotton ball wig and bloody Band-Aid sash. She dropped needle on warped vinyl. She climbed atop that enormous, intimidating stage. Bidet closed her eyes and began to sing. From the corners crept —

Curious rats and nosey spiders —
Alley cats and alligators —
Centipedes and rapt raccoons —
She harnessed the magic of that forsaken saloon.

Within months, a multitude of urban vermin cheered her on night-after-night. Predator and prey swayed side-by-side, allied within that safe space, and not only animals, but hobos too. Disheveled drunks tangoed with skunks, unsure if the merry menagerie was truly reality or simply the whiskey.

Success never smelled so sweet, and Bidet inhaled fully fame's fizzy bouquet. But she caught a whiff of something — rancid. At first she chose to ignore the faint taint, enjoy the party. This had been her dream, but her nose could not discount so obvious an aroma that every animal knows all too well. Closing night, and death was at the Poppycock's doorstep.

Bidet balanced atop a broken barstool and peered beyond boarded slats through stained, stained glass. The scavengers gathered just outside. Buzzards circled overhead. They wore cheap neckties and clutched crumpled contracts in their carroty claws. Up and down the boulevard, a corporate cancer grew inside the hollowed husks of hallowed LGBT hostelry.

Merchandise metastasized, growing like mold. Walls once tagged with graffiti glory were white washed away without delay. Rag doll shop girls sprouted like weeds and stitched happy smiles and button eyes onto condo buyers, who bled and bragged bout all the fun to be had in their clean new pads.

Those too poor to own were vacuum sealed in plastic, plucked like dog shit from the sidewalks, as malevolent yoga mommies mowed down slowpokes in their paths with razor-spoked baby strollers.

And Bidet gasped, because among the enemy were her idols — the Imperial Poppycock's previously disappeared poets, painters and performers. A generation of starving artists who'd survived the plague and grown fat, sucking on a Campbell's soup spoon, somehow blissfully unaware that "pop art" had become "big business."

Sell outs.

Hsssssst — cattle branded with corporate logos and paid with novelty oversized checks written out in the paltry amount of a few thousand Twitter followers.

Hssssssst!

Those daring downtown darlings, evil queens bereaved and deceived because they honestly believed the party was over? The protest had ended? That gay history died the night they left the scene? No offense, but Bidet was making gay history nightly. Where the fuck had they been?

They marched merrily, one by one, to a massive meat grinder where the rag dolls chewed them into commercial chum — artisanal tumor meat to feed the limousine liberals peering down from their penthouse palaces, unhappy it wasn't safe (yet) to go out at night. But so happy they'd bought-in — before the neighborhood had been discovered. Like when Columbus discovered America? The rent was practically a steal back then!

The doors of the Poppycock burst inward! Rag dolls dragged inside racks of dubious fashions. Vultures in hard hats with hammers busted down walls to open up the space. Chardonnay dilettantes day drank and swiped their plastic privilege, disposing of their garbage garments before they even left the store. The Imperial Poppycock Saloon was no more.

Years later, Bidet often joked that her fairy drag-mother had died — in childbirth.

The Imperial Poppycock Saloon had once been a bigger celebrity than any of the Hollywood luminaries who graced her doorstep. Yet it wasn't the drugs, the debauchery, or the even the opportunity to rub elbows with cabaret royalty — no. The Poppycock was so very loved because everyone from the millionaire movie stars to the bridge-and-tunnel Cinderellas, all the way down to the rats in the cellar — everyone under that roof was family. The Imperial Poppycock had been a mommy, daddy, gay uncle, lesbian auntie (and a fairy drag-mother) to so many.

It was why it was so very missed.

Americans don't like to contemplate death — at least not real death. Cartoon death? Slasher movie stab-stab-stabby death? Fairy tale death? Sure. Show us more! But not real death — the sort of death that takes you out of a work meeting, and your dad's on the phone. And he's crying. And you've never heard your father cry before. And quickly you gotta buy a plane ticket home, because the doctors aren't certain how much longer she has. That's real death.

For a humble rat such as Bidet, real death was simply a fact of real life — hell it was sometimes her next meal. But for us *thinking animals*, we require time. Time to process the pain. Time to heal the void that remains. Time to reflect on lessons we learned from the deceased, and sometimes the hardest lesson we learn from real death is that real life goes on. We awaken one morning, and suddenly we're the mommy, the daddy, the gay uncle and the lesbian auntie. And more times than not, the grandest means to honor a loved one's passing is by finding our own unique way to share of their legacy — to discover our own potential.

Now admittedly, it was cramped inside her pied-à-trashcan. Adding insult to injury were the falling bags of American Apparel intermittently interrupting a performance. *Absolute garbage.* Yet in spite of everything, everywhere Bidet looked, once again, life was on display:

There were club kid kitties and lesbian salamanders —
A bevy of beautiful burlesque beavers —
Hen party pigeons, chugging bubbly —
Hootin' and a'hollerin' at a Full Monty froggy —
Merry molly mice and hanky code hamsters —
Even an opossum DJ, just for good measure —
And a drag queen rat stood on a cigar box stage —
She proudly declared, "Welcome to Bidet's!"

18.

FANNY AND DOLORES

Shady Acres Nursing Home seemed like a fate worse than death. But following two weeks of self-imposed exile, hiding away within her barren bedroom, Dolores Diesel finally decided to give assisted living a try.

She was going to have to play Mahjong. *Fuck.*

The Mahjong room at *Shady Acres Nursing Home* was a blue-haired ocean of liver spotted biddies hunched over great walls of Chinese tiles. Dolores stomped from table to table in search of an open chair but was curtly denied over and over.

"Seat's taken."

"Occupied."

"We are full — *sorry.*"

A familiar fury rose hot and fast behind her bean bag breasts. Dolores hated being told *no.*

Boys play baseball?

Soldiers fight wars?

Men build skyscrapers?

Bullshit.

These fossilized bitches with their shared glances and little giggles deserved a knuckle sandwich. The heat in her chest burned away any scrap of good sense left in Dolores's head. Dentures were about to fly. When —

"Honey, over here. Come sit by me."

Dolores followed the sound of the voice. There, sitting all alone, was a curious old lady dolled up like a bordello madam: satin elbow gloves, sequined blue gown and a flowing feather boa. The woman's silver-auburn hair was a halo of fire and ice framing a delicate quilt of soft white wrinkles. Her emerald eyes sparkled like traffic lights on a snowy Chicago night. She was the prettiest dame Dolores had ever seen. Dolores sat down, suddenly (strangely) nervous, and introduced herself.

"Hello. I'm Dolores."

The pretty lady winked, "I'm Fanny." She then added, "Do you fucking hate Mahjong as much as I do?"

Confided Dolores, "Yes, very much so."

Fanny and Dolores chit-chatted right through Mahjong, Bingo, Uno and right into afternoon nap time. Dolores was quickly charmed by this eccentric septuagenarian with a flare for the dramatic. She learned that Fanny once worked for a world-renowned gypsy circus. She was their top billed performer known across the continent as the *Ruby of the Sky*. Then war came to Europe. The owners were secretly arrested in the middle of the night, charged with conspiracy. Fanny fled to America. She worked as a fashion model — then a photographer — in New York City. Businessmen lavished her with fur coats and French perfumes, but she denied every gesture. She leaned in close to Dolores and smirked, "No fat cat could ever clip my wings, honey. I reckon gals like us aren't the marrying type?"

Dolores got goose pimples. Was Fanny flirting with her? Lesbians their age were typically snooty bookkeepers, brittle as teacups. But Fanny was so worldly and sophisticated. Dolores — *not so much.*

She shared how she once built Army jeeps to help beat the Germans. She turned in her ratchet set for a hard hat, constructing iconic skyscrapers across a post-war America. Working with civilian men was sometimes a challenge. She'd try to chuckle as they cat-called another pretty lady walking past the construction yard. Inevitably, the chauvinism always came back around to wound her. Jokes about Dolores growing her hair out so she could "find herself a good husband" or insidious sarcasm concerning a gang of immigrant laborers "taking turns setting her straight." And the higher she climbed the harder those pigs tried to tear Dolores down.

"Bitch."

"Ballbuster."

"Dyke!"

To her credit, Dolores never stopped climbing, but she did stop smiling. A comfortable anger took root. Any askew glance was met with an atom bomb of profanities.

"Fuck yeah, I'm a dyke!"

Fanny seemed to sense Dolores' distress, "What say we go for a little stroll?"

The brisk winter walk proved soothing for Dolores. But now, something seemed to preoccupy Fanny's mind.

"Honey, I need to get something off my chest."

Dolores cut to the chase, "You're straight? Goddamnit, I'm so foolish."

Fanny laughed, "What? No. I'm gay as an ice cream social — and quite smitten with you." She paused. "Dolores, I'm a witch."

Fanny kissed Dolores on the cheek. Magic flowed between them. Reality was rewritten like the fleeting ripples of a pebble skipping across a placid pond. Gone was the January chill. In its place plinked far away wind chimes. The tinkling tapestry was accompanied by the smell of freshly mowed lawn and the tart taste of homemade pink lemonade. Two young girls tossed a baseball; they were Fanny and Dolores! Dolores's little hand barely fit the catcher's mitt, yet she threw that ball so high the heavens were awash with white weathered leather and red spinning stitching. The red bled into the white as the tom-girls tumbled into a freshly flowered field of crimson roses and scarlet carnations. They kissed ever so briefly as the flowers iced over and melted back to nothing. And there stood old, wrinkled Dolores holding old, wrinkled Fanny once more.

Dolores joked, "Well, a witch was my second guess."

And in that very moment, Dolores Diesel remembered how to smile.

Spring soon sprung at Shady Acres. Fanny and Dolores were quickly inseparable, giggling like *Golden Girl* schoolgirls. Dolores adored their daily ritual — she first to the cafeteria to give a standing ovation for Fanny's *fashionably late* arrival wearing another rhinestone chemise or fox fur stole. And Fanny opened Dolores's eyes to the witchery that weaved the world around them; the delicate balance of intention versus action; and how anger may feed one in the moment, but ultimately it's a cancer to the soul. Dolores rediscovered a youthful optimism she'd not felt in decades.

The summer days shortened — set against saffron hued shadows. Dolores stayed up late those autumn nights, whispering with Fanny over beeswax candles and keepsake mementos, listening as the pathetic phantom of a deceased neighbor bemoaned her desire not to depart but to stay — among her friends — to see her grandchildren one last time. Dolores watched with wonder as Fanny gently coaxed the frightened ghost from this world and into the weave beyond.

Fanny's private room at *Shady Acres* was a curated collection of colorful clutter, equal halves scrapbook and spell book. A vintage Ouija board hung alongside vibrant lithographs of lithe acrobats. Colorful scarves covered lamps, casting the room warmly as a gypsy campfire. A trailing tail of smoky incense lazily snaked in the spirit's woeful wake. And bedside, framed in silver, was a sepia splotched photo of a fire-haired young woman wearing a radiant unitard of dazzling diamonds. The *Ruby of the Sky* kissed Dolores upon her wrinkled lips.

"Let's fly, my love."

Dolores had never felt such exhilaration as Fanny's scarlet tresses whipped around them. *Shady Acres* was a fleeting memory as the witches climbed faster and steeper into the nighttime sky before coming to rest on the edge of a high wire perch. Both women now wore sparkly costumes and gilded tiaras. Dolores felt downright silly in the sapphire sausage casing, but she acquiesced, nonetheless, when Fanny ordered her to flourish. And the circus tent roared in approval!

Fanny handed the trapeze to Dolores, who now flew on her own, racing across oceans, over forests, through cities. She landed atop the steel beam of a skeletal skyscraper and sat down right next to Fanny, who tossed her a tuna sandwich from a rusted lunch pail. They wore grimy coveralls and hardhats. They chewed silently and gazed at the setting sun.

"Dolores, honey, you know my time is running out."

"Well, Fanny m'dear, let's make the most of what we have left."

Dusk became night. Planets and comets corkscrewed to create a cosmic kaleidoscope. A catwalk of ancient goddesses — Isis, Athena, Freya, Shakti — sashayed across the sky, accompanied by a celestial chorus of heavenly voices singing in celebration of sisterhood. That night, Dolores slept in Fanny's bed, but there was no sleeping to be had. They were a geriatric, orgiastic jigsaw puzzle of fingertips, lips, nipples and hips. They fucked — like fifty year olds!

Winter returned to *Shady Acres Nursing Home*. Fanny and Dolores shared practically every moment together, kissing goodnight as they went to their separate rooms and kicking off every morning with their adorable ritual. Dolores first to the cafeteria to admire Fanny's arrival in her fanciful finery. Until the morning Fanny did not make it to breakfast.

Dolores rushed to Fanny's room. She'd already been removed. She passed in her sleep. The nurses assured Dolores it'd been painless — quiet.

Dolores did not grieve. There'd be ample time for that. Instead, she gathered a box of books, candles — incense. She tucked that silver framed photo of the *Ruby of the Sky* beneath her arm, and Dolores Diesel retired to her room to wish her Fanny — farewell.

19.

CHA-CHA AND THE BLACK STAR

The reviews were in! Quote — "Cha-Cha the Caveman's comeback spectacular is nothing more than a rote exercise of bloated self-importance — an artist bereft of creativity — banking on name alone — utterly *Neanderthalic* in its execution." One star. ★

Cha-Cha swooned as though to faint. *Neanderthalic?* How was that even a criticism? He was a caveman. *Critics.*

In all honesty, there was no actual written review *per se.* The criticism more consisted of dung flung at pathetic Cha-Cha as he fled the fire pit following his final failed performance. Nonetheless, the tribe's disapproval stung Cha-Cha to his core. Artists are highly sensitive beings possessed of an emotional engagement that far, far outpaces an average person. (No offense.) And Cha-Cha, being the world's first artist, well he felt all the emotions — doubly so.

He felt resentment. He'd done so much for his tribe: invented theater, invented religion, invented cocaine, but nothing seemed good enough. He felt self doubt. Perhaps he should have written a funnier or simpler show — not so esoteric and sentimental? And Cha-Cha felt sadness, because he knew he had to leave. Besides, a younger entertainer had already taken Cha-Cha's place.

Her name was Cher. (It was Cher.) She went by *Cher-Cher* back then, totally stealing Cha-Cha's schtick. Nothing ever changes. There's always someone younger and hungrier waiting in the wings. It was barely the Stone Age and everything had already been done before.

So Cha-Cha packed his wheel, his magic hat and his sloth, and he ventured into the wilderness to find himself a new tribe — one who'd better appreciate him. Well, he quickly ate the sloth. The howling wind blew away his magic hat. And that fucking wheel was too heavy to roll through the snow. Stripped of every achievement, Cha-Cha nonetheless slogged onward, but the further he walked, the colder he felt. Cha-Cha eventually succumbed, slumping and shivering into the snow.

"Cha-Cha — wake up, sweet pea. I've been looking for you all day."

The little caveman opened his eyes to find a burly fellow standing above him. Dressed head to toe in cotton linen, snowy white as the gentleman's tangled beard. The stranger had the kindest eyes Cha-Cha'd ever seen.

Cha-Cha asked, "Are you — God?"

The stranger laughed, "Heavens no, Cha-Cha. God's in everything, not just a single person. Hell, I'm Walt Whitman."

It was poet and humanist, Walt Whitman!

"Now let's dust you off."

Cha-Cha's mastodon muumuu was matted with red dirt. He no longer stood in snow but atop rust colored sand, the signature shade of the planet Mars. Maroon dunes dotted the alien landscape in every direction, and straight ahead stood an intimidating Egyptian pyramid. Cha-Cha didn't recognize the stars overhead, but he did feel a particular kinship to a tiny blue jewel that sat just above the horizon.

"What is this place?"

"This is *Fancy*. It's a special place where only our most dignified — and deplorable — dames and dandies retire to help propagate human creativity. Now, you best get along to the party. Everyone's very excited for your arrival."

Cha-Cha passed through a Space Age archway and into a brightly lit salon where the most peculiar people buzzed about laughing and chatting. Every head turned when Cha-Cha entered the room.

"He's here!"

A jewelry laden Liberace tickled the ivories as Factory femme fatale Holly Woodlawn threw open a space porthole and screamed to the stars, "Free pussy, motherfuckers!"

(Nobody knows how to kick off a party quite like Holly.)

Speaking of the Factory, Andy Warhol was not speaking to Oscar Wilde — again. The two had another terrible tiff, this time over who'd get Cha-Cha as their newest muse. Everyone took sides. Willi Ninja challenged Oscar to a vogue battle, and Joan of Arc wounded Warhol with her sword — *my word*. The conflict got so epic that Shakespeare penned thirteen dramatic comedies. (Or were they *comedic dramadies?*) Each one starring teensy Klaus Nomi as Garglespunks the Clown and Divine as Empress Enema, who (spoiler alert) poo-poo's the entire proposal by appointing herself muse-in-perpetuity to both the sparring popinjays.

Cha-Cha found all the fuss incredibly confusing.

"You look lost, baby," lisped Paul Lynde as he took center square of hot new game show *Dead Hollywood Queers*.

He added, "Sit to my left, Cha-Cha. You'll make my bad side look better."

They were joined by Noël Coward, Coco Chanel, Plato, James Baldwin, Lord Byron, Keith Haring and Alan Turing. The quiz show hostess was infamous Hollywood actress Joan Crawford. And Paul seethed with envy when

Turing won instantly. But honestly, it didn't take a hero codebreaker to determine the answer to every query would be: "No. Wire. Hangers!"

Lithe and limber, Alvin Ailey spun Cha-Cha across the dance floor over to nightlife legend Leigh Bowery, who shimmied seductively with Freddie Mercury. Truman Capote mopped himself with a perfumed hanky.

"Is the heat on? Langston, sweetie? Are ya hot?"

Langston Hughes was not hot. He was, however, sick of Capote's complaining. So he introduced Cha-Cha to his good friend Sylvester, who took Cha-Cha to a cabaret stage where he asked him, "Do you wanna funk?"

Cha-Cha wanna funk!

And funk he did, all night long, flanked on either side by the funkiest, the fanciest, glamour gods of rock and roll — Prince and Bowie!

A shower of glitter, granite and choking confetti engulfed the stage that rocked up and down as seismic applause rocked Cha-Cha like a megaton bomb!

"Cha-Cha!"

"Cha-Cha!"

"Cha-Cha!"

"Chaaaaaaaaaaaaaaaaaaaaaaa!"

20.

NUMBER TWENTY

Professor Gif Jeffries addressed the lecture hall:

"Among the twenty-six Neanderthals identified at the Craswell Crags dig site, *Number Twenty* stands out for the completeness of its skeleton, perfectly preserved beneath a delicate crush of limestone and calcium silicate — the result of the ancient earthquake that collapsed the cavern.

"Points of interest include the specimen's small size. An adult male, but barely larger than the females of its species, its bones describe a brutal existence, with multiple healed fractures suggesting abuse from the larger males.

"But most intriguing is *Twenty's* ornamentation. Found inside its alcove were pigmented shells, pottery, primitive jewelry, and even a flap of leather our team strongly believes is — a hat. The first example of such apparel discovered during the Late Pleistocene. This leads us to conclude that *Twenty* possessed symbolic thinking and likely served the tribe in some ceremonial capacity.

"Call me a romantic, but the very origin of human mythology may well be buried by his side.

"Sweet dreams, little guy.

ABOUT THE AUTHOR

Dandy Darkly is the painted, pontificating performance artist best known for his immersive storytelling that blends cabaret and spoken word with bespoke musical compositions and eclectic sound effects to create an utterly unique audience experience. To date, Dandy has produced four critically acclaimed solo shows at the Edinburgh Festival Fringe with additional performances at the New Orleans Fringe, Frigid New York, the Queerly Festival, the National Steampunk Festival and the London Horror Festival. New York City's East Village is Dandy's playground with neo-vaudeville cavalcades at Under St. Marks Theater, the Slipper Room, Dixon Place and Stonewall Inn along with London's Royal Vauxhall Tavern. Dandy also hosts an annual secret performance every Bear Week down under Provincetown's infamous Dick Dock. In 2017, Dandy takes off on a multi-city US tour including Chicago, Orlando, Tampa, Providence, San Francisco and more. For additional information visit dandydarkly.com and follow Dandy on Twitter @dandydarkly.

"Never be too afraid to laugh." Dandy Darkly